Alberto
GIACOMETTI

Why
I am
a sculptor

FONDATION-
GIACOMETTI

hermann
Depuis 1876

Notes sur la sculpture.

Je ne peux parler qu'indirectement de mes sculptures et chercher à dire ce qui les a provoquées.
Depuis des années je n'ai réalisé que les sculptures qui se présentaient toutes finies dans mon esprit, je les recopiais dans l'espace sans rien y changer, sans aucune modification, sans me demander ce qu'elles pouvaient signifier. (Il me suffit de devoir y changer une partie, chercher une dimension pour que je sois complètement perdu et tout l'objet s'abolit. Je ne vois jamais rien sous forme de tableau, rarement de dessin et ça me trouble beaucoup, les efforts constants que j'ai fait quelquefois pour réaliser un tableau ou toujours complètement échoué.))

Une sculpture finie je crois y voir, transformés et déplacés des images, des faits, des émotions qui m'ont profondément impressionné et des formes que je sens m'être très près mais que je ne comprends pas (je dois dire que les objets que je ne peux le plus définir sont ceux qui m'expliquent, qui m'enveloppent ou m'étonnent me semblent les plus près et les plus vivant.

Je veux citer en tout par exemple la sculpture reproduite ici et qui représente un palais ☆

(Cet objet s'est formé peu à peu (été-automne 1932) en hiver il devenait plus clair, les différentes parties prenaient leurs places, leurs formes exactes et en automne tout avait pris telle réalité que dans une journée je pouvais le fabriquer dans l'espace.

Cette sculpture se rapporte complètement à l'époque merveilleuse qui prenait fin une année plus tôt, on pendant 6 mois j'ai passé chaque heure à côté d'une femme qui concentrant en elle-même toute la vie rendait chaque instant merveilleux pour moi. Nous construisions un fantastique palais dans la nuit (les jours et les nuits avaient la même couleur, la lumière du petit matin, je n'ai jamais vu le soleil pendant cette époque) un palais très fragile en allumettes, au moindre faux mouvement des parties s'écroul...

finish the sculptures, make 2 new ones, exhibit them.
<u>write</u>,

Notebooks, 1933-1934

I can only speak *indirectly* of my sculptures

The Palace at 4 a.m., 1932
Photo Man Ray

I can only speak *indirectly* of my sculptures, and can only in part hope to express what motivated them.

For years I have only made the sculptures that presented themselves to my mind in a finished state, merely reproducing them in space without changing any aspect of them or wondering what they could mean (suffice it for me to begin to modify one of their parts, or to seek a certain dimension, to find myself completely at a loss and the whole object destroyed). Nothing ever appeared before me in the form of a picture, I seldom see in the form of a drawing. The attempts at conscious execution of a painting or even of a sculpture, to which I have occasionally surrendered, have always failed.

Once the object has been constructed, I have a tendency to rediscover in it — transformed and displaced — images, impressions, facts which have deeply moved me (often without my knowing it), forms which I feel are very close to me, although I am often unable to identify them, which makes them more disturbing to me.

I take the sculpture reproduced opposite for instance, which represents a palace. The object was created, piece by piece, at the end of summer 1932 and slowly became clear to me, its different parts acquiring their exact shapes and their precise place in the ensemble. By the autumn it had become so real that its execution in space required no more than one day's work.

It no doubt refers to the stage in my life that had concluded a year earlier, a period of six months spent hour after hour with a woman who, concentrating all life in herself, made every moment something marvellous for me.

We used to construct a fantastic palace in the night (days and nights were the same colour as if everything had happened just before dawn; throughout this time I never saw the sun), a very fragile palace of matchsticks: at the slightest false move a whole part of the minute construction would collapse: we would always begin it again. I don't know why it is filled with a spinal column in a cage — the spinal column which this woman sold me on one of the first nights I met her in the street — and by one of the skeleton birds she saw the very night preceding the morning on which our life together broke down — the skeleton birds fluttering way above the reservoir of clear green water in which the very delicate and very white skeletons of fishes were swimming, in the grand open-air hall amid the exclamations of astonishment at four o'clock in the morning. In the middle, the scaffolding of a tower which is perhaps unfinished, or perhaps the whole of its top has fallen in, been broken. The statue of a woman has occupied the other side, a woman in whom I discover my mother, as she appears in my earliest memories. I was troubled by her long black dress, which touched the ground: it seemed to be part of her body, and this frightened and confused me; all the rest was lost on me. That figure stands out three times against the same curtain, and onto that curtain

I opened my eyes for the first time. Captive of an infinite charm, I stared at that brown curtain under which a thin strip of light was filtered, all along the floor.

I can say nothing of the object on a small red board; I feel identified with it.

Minotaure, n° 3-4, 12 December 1933

Henri Laurens
by Alberto Giacometti

to Mrs Laurens

Once again today, on the first day of the year, I'm trying to write the text that's been occupying my mind almost exclusively for one week now, but each day the difficulty of finding words, of constructing sentences, of succeeding in composing a whole piece is becoming greater. Yesterday, I was sobbing inside with rage facing the total deficiency of my means of expression, facing those laconic, weightless sentences that don't express at all what I mean to say. However, I must try to do it well. The evening Skira asked me if I wanted to write this article, I didn't give a precise answer, but, almost immediately, I was taken over by a multitude of images that all referred to the region that is Laurens and his work. I no longer paid attention to what was being said at our table and for the whole evening, those images haunted me.

I could see, I could feel the bright street at eleven in the morning, "I'm going to Laurens", the yellow trees of the Villa Brune, the railway embankment. The high grey door of the studio. My anxiety at the moment of knocking "What if he's not at home?", my disappointment caused by the silence that persists, my joy on hearing steps approaching on the other side. Laurens' smile, the colour, the volume of his head at the moment the sculptures, in front of me, barely perceived, please my gaze.
Seen from behind, Laurens, one evening at dusk, walks

in the rue Saint-Benoît. The green leaves, a sentence said by him as he went by car to Mrs Laurens, in the countryside: "Here's our old house". The nice feeling generated by the relations of height and width when first seeing a work by Laurens. The immediate certainty: "This sculpture is very good once and for all."

Among those images, there is especially one that came back, imposed itself and gradually took the place of all the others, the only one that had no direct relation to reality.

I could see myself in a strange clearing, a vaguely circular space whose main colour was autumn leaves, whose quite close limits were lost in an atmosphere at the same time dense and light, and very soft. Around me sprang up, thirty centimetres above the ground and unevenly scattered, strange little hills that alternated with indefinable constructions, whitish, evoking small castles seen through a curtain of steam. But those hills, those constructions were complex, surrounded with resonances, and I could feel they were gestures, sounds of voices, movements, marks, sensations that had been, once, far from one another, in time, in the course of all those years.

Now those sensations became objects, simultaneously existed in the space around me and *filled me with delight*.

I first took them for my own memories, but yesterday, trying to write what I experienced in front of Laurens'

Tyler

A CHRISTMAS NOVEL

ANGEL INSTITUTE
BOOK ONE

LUCY MCCONNELL

Copyright © 2024 by Lucy McConnell

All rights reserved.

No part of this book may be reproduced in any form or by any electronic or mechanical means, including information storage and retrieval systems, without written permission from the author, except for the use of brief quotations in a book review.

Dear Reader,

We're so delighted you're here! Welcome to Angel Institute, where romance, Christmas magic, and angels-in-training come together to share the Spirit of Christmas right in the heart of Benton Falls.

This series draws inspiration from some of the most beloved Christmas classics, including—but certainly not limited to—*It's a Wonderful Life*, *A Christmas Carol*, *White Christmas*, and, of course, the greatest story ever told—the birth of our Savior, Jesus Christ, when angels proclaimed tidings of great joy.

As you journey through these stories, we hope you'll feel the wonder of the season, the warmth of love for your family and sweetheart, and, most importantly, the deep love God has for you.

Heaven is always mindful of you, dear friend. There are angels all around you, cheering you on and working for your good. Our prayer is that as you read, you'll recognize their presence, feel their support, and rejoice with them this Christmas.

Merry Christmas!

Lucy & Erica

Prologue

ROSE

I'm a guardian angel in training.
It's not what you think it is.
Basically, I take classes that are really hard to sit through. They're not hard for some angels in our class. Lillian, the angel who works in the library, has no trouble sitting still. She's calm and full of peace. I'm peaceful—er, at peace with me, who I am, and where I'm going.

I'm just the type of angel who likes to keep moving.

Henry, our instructor, doesn't seem to mind my constantly tapping toes. He likes moving things like cogs and wheels and such. Sometimes, I wonder if he sees our class as one big clock—all the parts moving at just the right time, making small adjustments that create big results.

We all have a unique way of looking at our life after death.

Henry's is like a clock.

Mine is like a dance. Each movement progresses smoothly into the next one. Some steps are easier to combine, while others take practice.

I guess life on Earth can be like that, too.

I wrote a whole paper on the subject. But that was last semester.

This semester is all about practical application, and today is a very big day for us because we're getting our final assignments.

And by assignment, I mean human assignment.

This is the big leagues.

Real children of God who need heaven's help.

I'm so nervous I could eat a hippo.

Not really. Angels don't eat hippos. It's a saying I picked up somewhere. I rather like it because it's ridiculous. God has a sense of humor, you know.

I glance around to see if anyone else is as nervous as I am. Our classroom is lovely. As much as I don't like sitting in a desk, I do like it here. The walls shimmer with soft golds and silvers, and the ceiling above twinkles with stars that seem to wink encouragingly at us. More than once, I looked up at them and found the answer I was searching for.

My gaze sweeps across the room, taking in the familiar faces of my fellow angels–in–training. We've been through so much together; our bond forged through marathon study sessions and shared hopes.

Henry stands at the front of the room, his wings folded majestically behind him.

Oh, the wings!

Being a guardian angel is a calling and a purpose we all attain to, but I can't wait to get my wings because they're stunning. Think of the dance moves I could do with those. The choreography. I stop myself from daydreaming about that right now. This moment is too important to miss. I wiggle in my seat and sit taller.

Henry's twinkling blue eyes and messy silver hair give him an air of both wisdom and mischief. Sometimes, I wonder what kind of angel in training he was.

"Welcome, my dear trainees," Henry begins, his voice warm and comforting. Thank goodness angels don't sleep—his voice would put me out in a jiffy. "I have your assignment letters right here." He waves his hand over a stack of envelopes. There's no such thing as cheap paper in heaven. Every scrap of parchment is of the highest quality, and our letters are no exception.

Henry pauses, a small smile playing at the corners of his mouth. "I should tell you that you'll be going down during the Christmas season."

Rebecca, her hair so white it's almost translucent, straightens up beside me. "Christmas? That'll be amazing. It's the best season of the year to bring hope." Her grin is infectious as she looks around at us. "Angels are always welcome during Christmas."

I nod in agreement, my toes tapping out a quiet beat of excitement. The scent of cinnamon and pine seems to waft through the air at the mere mention of the holiday, and I can almost hear the distant jingling of sleigh bells.

Henry's smile grows wider, but there's a hint of caution in his eyes. "There will be goodwill on Earth, and brotherly love spread from person to person. Christmas is a wonderful time of the year. It also adds an element to your assignments that's... tricky."

My tapping rhythm falters for a moment as Rebecca gives him a questioning look. "How so?"

He clears his throat as if the words got stuck there, and he has to make himself say something unpleasant. "Many of your assignments are in danger of losing the Christmas Spirit forever."

The weight of his words settles over us like a heavy blanket, and my leg that always bounces, stops.

Lillian, her eyes wide, starts to speak, "That means —."

"It means that your intervention is important in God's plan for these people." Henry's gaze meets each of ours in turn, and when his eyes lock with mine, I feel a surge of determination rush through me.

As Henry continues explaining the details of our assignments, I tap my toes three times. The chance to make a real difference, to help someone rediscover the Spirit of Christmas, is everything I've been training for.

The stakes are so high, and not just for our assignments. If we fail, we'll have to wait a hundred years to try again to become guardian angels.

My thoughts drift to my assignment, wondering who I'll be tasked to help. As Henry begins handing out the letters, I close my eyes for a moment, offering up a silent prayer. 'Please,' I think, 'let me be the angel this person needs.'

When Henry reaches me, his eyes soften. He places the letter on my desk, and I feel its weight—not just physical, but spiritual, too. It's too big for my hands to pick up.

"Henry?" I ask quietly, hoping my fellow students don't hear. "Will you open it with me after class?"

He nods and keeps walking.

I lean away from the envelope. It's not just my future in there; it's that of a child of God's future. I'm too young of an angel to be given this kind of responsibility, and I want to run from the room and everything it represents.

Around me, my fellow angels–in–training are reacting to their own assignments. Rebecca sighs dramatically about weather forecasting, while Lillian grins at the prospect of guiding lost souls.

Henry's final words of advice bring me back to the present. "Remember, you are never alone. You can call the Blessing Hotline at any time and pray to the Father. I'm around if you need me, please ask for help. Class dismissed."

Everyone rises from their seats. Some have quiet conversations as they discuss their assignments. Others march off, determined to make a difference.

I put my hand over the letter and slide it across the desk and then up to my chest. "Okay, Rose," I whisper, "time to face the music. Let's hope your steps are light enough to dance your way through this assignment.

"You coming?" Rose asks.

I shake my head. "I need to talk to Henry."

"Okay. Be blessed." She grins and heads out, holding all the optimism in the world in her hands.

I sit on my desk, my toes tapping on the chair.

When the room clears, Henry comes to stand next to my desk. "Are you ready?"

"No," I tell him truthfully. "Is anyone ever ready? I mean, everyone else seemed ready to jump in, so maybe it's just me."

"Rose," Henry removes his gold-rimmed glasses. "You wouldn't be here if He didn't think you were ready."

I draw a breath. "I know."

Henry points to the envelope. "Why don't you open that?"

I slip my finger under the seal and pause. *I can do all things through Him who created me*; I repeat the phrase to myself. "Here goes nothin'."

Dear Guardian Angel Trainee,

This Christmas season, you are tasked with a mission of utmost importance —one that will determine your readiness to receive your wings and ascend to the honored rank of guardian angel.

You are hereby assigned to:
Tyler Olsen, a lawyer

Your objective is to help Tyler discover and embrace the true spirit of family this Christmas. This task will require all the skills and compassion you have cultivated during your training at the Angel Institute.

Be advised: the stakes are high. If you succeed in your mission, Tyler will be able to spend future Christmases with his daughter, creating cherished memories and strengthening their bond. However, if you fail, Tyler risks losing this precious opportunity and will face lonely Christmases ahead.

May the light of Heaven guide you in this crucial endeavor. We have the utmost faith in your abilities.

Wishing you divine success,
The Angelic High Council

ONE MIRACLE

I glance up after reading the letter. "I'm not even sure where to start." How does one go about teaching a workaholic to let go of the things he thinks are important?

"Let's go see what Tyler's life is like, shall we?" he asks. "Then we can discuss your approach."

I nod, and we move to Tyler's office, invisible to him but able to take in all around us.

The scene is so vivid I can almost smell the stale coffee and feel the tension radiating from Tyler's hunched shoulders.

As we watch, I take in every detail of Tyler's appearance. His rugged features are set in a mask of concentration; his brow furrowed as he pores over legal documents. A five o'clock shadow darkens his jaw, and his brown eyes, though focused, carry a hint of weariness.

"He works so hard," I murmur, my heart aching for the obvious strain etched into every line of Tyler's face.

Henry nods solemnly. "Indeed. Tyler believes that by burying himself in work, he can provide the best life for his daughter. But in doing so, he's missing out on the most precious gift of all—time with her."

I watch as Tyler glances at a framed photo on his desk. Even from our heavenly vantage point, I can see the love that softens his features as he looks at the image of a smiling little girl with golden curls and bright blue eyes.

"That's Leena," Henry explains. "Tyler's world revolves around her, even if he struggles to show it sometimes."

As the hours tick by, Tyler remains at his desk, the stack of papers seeming never to diminish. The office grows darker, shadows creeping in from the corners, but Tyler barely notices. He reaches for his coffee mug, grimacing as he sips the cold, bitter liquid.

"Doesn't he realize how late it's getting?" I ask, frustration coloring my voice. "Surely Leena is waiting for him at home."

Henry's expression is sympathetic. "Tyler's fear of failure, of not being enough for Leena, drives him to work beyond reason. He believes that financial security will make up for the emotional distance he's created."

I shake my head, my heart heavy with the weight of Tyler's misguided efforts. "But she's just a little girl."

"Precisely," Henry agrees. "And if he doesn't change, he'll lose her, lose his sense of family gathering together to celebrate Christmas, and spend every holiday alone."

"No!" I whisper.

"Help him, Rose. Help him see what a treasure he has, so he doesn't lose it forever," Henry encourages me.

Tyler finally looks at the clock. His eyes widen in surprise, and he hurriedly begins to pack up his things. I can sense the guilt radiating from him as he realizes how late it's gotten.

"He's heading home now," I observe. "Can we follow him?"

Henry nods, and with another wave of his hand, the scene before us shifts. We're now watching Tyler as he hurries down the street. The contrast between the festive decorations adorning the buildings and Tyler's dejected posture is stark. He doesn't look like he belongs with the happy shoppers and families out to see the lights in the town square.

"He's missing it all," I whisper, my heart aching for the joy Tyler is denying himself.

Henry's voice is gentle as he replies, "Sometimes, Rose, the hardest hearts to reach are those that have been hurt the most. Tyler's pain blinds him to the wonder of the season. He doesn't let himself feel anything because he might feel things that hurt."

Tyler approaches his home, which is a modest but well-kept house without one decoration out front. A teenage girl comes out the front door, her coat done up like she's been waiting for the chance to go.

"Good evening, Mr. Olsen," she says. "Leena's already in bed. She tried to wait up for you, but…"

Tyler nods, his guilt evident in the slump of his shoulders. "Thank you, Sarah. I'm sorry for keeping you so late again."

Sarah gives him a sympathetic smile. "It's no trouble. Leena did want you to read her a bedtime story…"

I can almost feel Tyler's heart constrict at those words. He fumbles in his pocket, pulling out some cash. "Here, for the extra time. I appreciate your help."

Sarah accepts the money with a nod. "Goodnight, Mr. Olsen."

As Sarah walks away, Tyler stands for a moment on the porch, his hand on the doorknob. I can sense the turmoil within him–the desire to be the father Leena deserves warring with his fear of not being enough.

"Oh, Tyler," I murmur, wishing I could reach out and comfort him. "You're enough. You just need to believe it."

Henry places a comforting hand on my shoulder.

We follow Tyler inside. The house is messy. The dishes are done, but there are coloring books and toys strewn about. Blankets are thrown wherever they were last used, and it looks like popcorn pieces are strewn about in front of the television.

After a moment's hesitation, Tyler begins to climb the stairs. My heart lifts, hoping he'll seize this opportunity to connect with his daughter.

As he gently pushes open Leena's bedroom door, I feel a surge of love so pure it takes my breath away. Leena is curled up in her bed, her golden curls spread out on the pillow like a halo. A book lies open on the bedside table–"The Night Before Christmas."

Tyler moves quietly to her bedside, gently brushing a curl from her forehead. Leena stirs at his touch, her blue eyes fluttering open.

"Daddy?" she murmurs sleepily. "You're home."

"Hey, princess," he whispers, sitting on the edge of her bed. "I'm sorry I missed story time."

Leena sits up, rubbing her eyes. "It's okay, Daddy. Can you read to me now?"

The hope in her voice is impossible to resist. Tyler hesitates for just a moment before nodding. "Of course."

As Tyler begins to read "The Night Before Christmas," his rich voice bringing the classic tale to life, I feel a warmth spread through my celestial form, letting me know that this is right, this is truth—it's Tyler's truth.

I watch as Leena snuggles closer to her father, her eyes wide with wonder as she listens to the story. Tyler's voice grows more animated as he reads, and I can see the stress of the day melting away from his features.

"Look, Henry," I whisper, my voice filled with awe. "Do you see it?"

Henry nods, a knowing smile on his face. "This is the man Tyler could be–the father he wants to be. Your job is to help him become this version of himself, not just in these fleeting moments, but in every aspect of his life."

As Tyler finishes the story, Leena is fighting to keep her eyes open. He tucks her in, placing a gentle kiss on her forehead.

"Goodnight, Daddy," Leena murmurs. "I love you."

"I love you too, princess," Tyler replies. "Sweet dreams."

As Tyler quietly leaves the room, I can sense the conflict within him. The love he feels for Leena is overwhelming, but so is his fear of failing her.

I square my shoulders, determination filling me. I'm not scared anymore. "I won't let them down, Henry. I'll help Tyler see the truth and bring this family together before Christmas Eve."

As we watch Tyler retreat to his study, once again burying himself in work, I can feel the weight of my mission settling upon me. It won't be easy to break through Tyler's walls to help him overcome his fears and embrace the joy of family and the Christmas season.

I may be a guardian angel in training, but I'm determined to earn my wings and bring the true spirit of Christmas to Tyler and Leena. Miracles are possible. And that's exactly what this family needs—a Christmas miracle.

One

TYLER

A chaotic symphony of chatter, holiday music, papers moving, children running, and chairs scraping against the wood floor one-hundred percent overruns me as I step into the elementary school gymnasium. I'm used to the busy noises of an office full of adults where the loudest thing in the room is the copy machine that never sleeps. The constant *beep-click-click--whirl* is comforting. It means work is getting done.

There's always work to do.

I have two depositions, three legal briefs, and seven court pleadings to finish before the end of the day. My fingers itch to get started and the legalese circles in my mind on a constant loop even as I navigate time with my daughter.

Above the doorway is a sign that reads "Winter Wonderland," and I can't help but wonder who came up with that advertising gimmick. Wonderland? More like

Winter Pandemonium. If there is such a thing as controlled chaos, this is not it. Whose idea was it to bring together vast numbers of unruly children and glitter?

A pathetic few strands of lights are strung across the ceiling. A large Christmas tree stands in the center of the room, decorated by the third and fourth graders. It looks like the tree had a red and green sneezing fit.

I take a deep breath, trying to center myself amidst the chaos and choke on the scent of Elmer's glue, which is so thick it coats my lungs.

"Daddy, look!" Leena tugs on my sleeve, her blue eyes wide with wonder. "Can we go see Santa?"

I glance at the long line snaking its way toward Santa's grotto in the corner, my heart sinking at the thought of standing there for who knows how long. "Maybe a little later, princess. Why don't we look at some of the crafts first?" I hold up the tickets we bought at the door. Each ticket gets us a chance at a craft table. Just seconds ago, Leena insisted that she wanted to do them all. How could I resist? It's not like I'm going to do all this stuff with her at home. This is kind of our one shot at crafting this season.

Not that I spent all that much time crafting in my life. My mom used to love it, though. I should call her.

"Come on!" Leena pulls on my arm, dragging me from table to table, her face alight with joy at each new option. Her enthusiasm is infectious, and I feel a smile tugging at the corners of my mouth despite my initial reluctance to attend this event. *This is why I'm here*, I remind myself. For Leena.

My phone buzzes in my pocket. I pull it out, recognizing the number of one of my most demanding clients. There's no way I can put him off without major backlash. With a sigh, I answer the call. "Tyler Olsen speaking."

As I listen to my client ramble about a last-minute contract change, I try to keep an eye on Leena. She's moved on to a table where they make reindeer ornaments out of popsicle sticks. I nod along to the voice in my ear, only half-listening as I watch my daughter.

"You'd better have it taken care of before tomorrow morning!" he snaps.

"I understand the urgency," I say, pinching the bridge of my nose. "I'll review the changes and get back to you."

It's always a balancing act, trying to be both a successful lawyer and a father. More often than not, I feel like I'm failing at both. If I could just make a partner, then things would lighten up. I frown, thinking about the partners at the firm. They play golf. They go out for long lunches. But more often than not, they're in the office as long as I am.

"Daddy, can I make one of these?" Leena asks, pointing to the paper snowflakes a couple of tables over.

"Of course, sweetheart," I reply, handing her a couple of tickets.

I wish I could be more like Leena. Despite everything she's been through—losing her mother and adjusting to life with just me—she still approaches each day with such enthusiasm that I'm exhausted the moment she wakes up. I wish I could bottle up some of that for myself. Heck, if I could bottle and sell it to other exhausted parents, I'd be a millionaire.

We find two empty seats at the craft table, and I help Leena get settled with a sheet of white paper and a pair of safety scissors. As she begins carefully folding her paper, her tongue poking out in concentration. The stage at the far end of the gym catches my eye. It's set up for a holiday performance later, with a painted backdrop of a snowy village made from those giant rolls of butcher paper schools love.

Suddenly, a flash of chestnut curls near the stage draws my attention, and I find myself locking eyes with a familiar face across the crowded room. A thrill shoots through my veins and I'm more awake now than when I raced to the car in the snow without my coat.

Gabby Robinson.

Her name is cute–like her. I wonder if it's short for Gabrielle or Abigail or some other more formal version her parents assigned her at birth. I shake my head. Her legal name is none of my concern.

Gabby is Leena's orchestra teacher. We've had a couple of parent-teacher conferences where she told me how wonderful Leena is, and I completely agree with her. Leena is learning to play the violin, and I'm grateful she practices with her after-school babysitter before I get home.

She's wearing a pair of jeans that hug all the right curves and a bright green sweater that works with her complexion. It's a unique color–which is probably why

I'm still staring at her, even though she's now focused on the group of children surrounding her, clutching various instruments. From this distance, I can see the warmth in her hazel eyes as she smiles encouragingly. Something inside me stirs, a feeling I haven't experienced in years.

Interest.

For a brief moment, I allow myself to really look at her. Her cheeks are flushed, and her hair falls in soft waves around her animated face. She looks at each student as they ask questions and gives them her full attention. I want to have some of that attention. I stand before judges, lawyers, and jurors, every one of them either waiting to trip me up or confirm my words, staring at me with complete attention–and I don't feel like those kids. They feel important. They stand taller, they smile wide, they nod along as she talks to them...

What would it be like to have her look at me like I matter?

As if sensing my gaze, she looks up, and our eyes meet across the room.

The connection lasts only a second, but it's enough to send an unexpected jolt through my stomach. I quickly avert my gaze. Maybe I'm not ready for that kind of focus.

What am I doing? I chastise myself silently. *I don't have time for... whatever that was.*

"Look, Daddy!" Leena exclaims, holding up her completed snowflake. It's still square, and the holes aren't even. "Isn't it pretty?"

"It's beautiful, princess," I say, pushing thoughts of Gabby from my mind. "Just like you."

Leena beams at me. She's done here and ready to move on. My phone buzzes again. I pull it out with a sigh, seeing a work email that needs my attention. I scan it. Shoot. Where did I file that report?

CRASH!

My head snaps up. A table of plastic bauble ornaments has toppled, sending glitter and balls bouncing across the floor. Leena stands in the middle of the chaos, her eyes wide with shock and brimming with tears. I'm not even sure how such a small child was able to knock over the whole table.

"I'm sorry!" she wails as I rush to her side. "I didn't mean to!"

The vendor, a kind-faced older woman, is already bending down to start cleaning up. "It's alright, dear," she says soothingly. "Accidents happen."

Leena turns into my shoulder, her tears soaking through my button-up shirt. She's getting messy and trying hard not to cry out loud.

I can't shake the guilt that's settling in my stomach. If I hadn't been distracted by work, if I had been paying closer attention... The familiar self-doubt creeps in, whispering that I'm not cut out for this, that I'm failing Leena just like I failed in my marriage.

"Let's help clean up. Okay?" I ask gently. "No one is mad at you, princess."

She sniffles and then pulls away.

I tuck my phone in my pocket.

"Here, let me help." I look up to see Gabby kneeling across from us. She's even prettier up close. Not that I'm noticing.

Leena sniffs and nods at her, too. Her eyes are red, and her chin seems glued to her chest. Gabby hands her several baubles. "Did I ever tell you about the time I knocked over my grandma's Christmas tree and smashed her glass ornaments?"

Leena shakes her head.

Gabby talks as we work. The older woman sits herself back at the table, rubbing her right knee. She lifts her shoulders at me as if saying, "It's no fun getting old." I copy her gesture not sure what I'm saying back. I lift the table and notice that the one leg won't sit straight. I have to yank it hard into place. That's probably why Leena was able to knock it down. I make sure it's stable before moving back to the clean-up crew.

The baubles are easy to gather, but the glitter is another thing. My pants, my palms, and my tie are covered in it. I dash off for a broom and dustpan. When I get back, Gabby is almost done with her story, and Leena smiles at me.

I mouth *thank you* to Gabby.

She smiles, and my embarrassment over being in the middle of chaos settles just like that.

"I'm scheduled to be at this booth before the concert," she tells us, though she's focused on Leena. "Will you help me teach the kindergarteners how to decorate these?" She holds up a clear bauble.

Leena nods, already forgetting that she was clumsy

and feeling more like an experienced, knowledgeable third-grader who can bestow her wisdom on little kids.

Before I knew it, we were the most popular ornament table in the gym. Several kids gather around, and Leena shows them how to squeeze the glue to make designs that they can then glitter up. '

I'm pushed to the back of the table to make room for more children to work. I have to watch where I step. Was Leena this small? I move back another step and bump into someone. Spinning, I find myself face-to-face with Gabby. Up close, I can see the light dusting of freckles across her nose. "Thank you," I say, suddenly feeling a bit tongue-tied. "For helping with... all of this."

Gabby's smile widens. "It was my pleasure, Mr. Olsen." She places her hand on my arm and I lose feeling in half of my body. "Or... may I call you Tyler?"

"Tyler is fine," I reply, acutely aware of the warmth in her gaze and that she's paralyzed me with a touch. "Uh." I have no words. There is nothing in my head except this fuzzy, wonderful feeling that makes it impossible to speak.

"Are you staying for the concert?" she asks.

Concert? I glance at the stage where kids organize music on stands while carrying instruments under their arms. Part of me wants to make an excuse, to retreat to the safety of our quiet home where work and responsibilities await, but the warmth of Gabby's invitation makes me pause. Is it possible she wants me to stay? Not just so they have bodies in the seats, but because she wants *me* here?

"Please!" Leena exclaims, bouncing on her toes.

Perfect! I don't have to answer my own question and have an excuse to linger. On the one hand, Gabby could think I'm supporting her efforts. On the other, she could think I was giving in to my daughter's whim. Interpretation is a tricky thing when it comes to law, but in this situation, it works in my favor. "Alright then, I guess we're staying."

Gabby lifts her shoulders as she breathes in, as if soaking up this moment. I get the feeling she's happy with my answer, and I give her a one-sided smile that always got me dates in college.

And this is where my lawyer brain kicks in, and interpretation turns around and sticks its tongue out at me.

Is she happy because *I'm* staying at her request?

Is she happy because I did something for my daughter and prioritized her?

Is she happy to have people here for her students to play in front of?

Or is she just happy to share Christmas music with the world?

Oh, interpretation, you sneaky devil you.

Students begin to warm up their instruments, and Gabby jolts. "Come sit up front," she urges. She touches my arm again as she brushes past me.

That was definitely a flirty touch. Even I can't misinterpret that signal.

As we make our way towards the chairs, the crowd seems to part around her, as if she carries her own bubble of calm amidst the chaos of the fair.

"So," she says, her voice carrying a hint of amusement, "are you enjoying the craft fair so far?"

I let out a small laugh. "Well, it's been... eventful. But Leena seems to be having a great time, so I guess that's what matters. We don't do things like this at home." I wave my arm toward the cotton-ball snowman station.

Gabby's eyes soften. "It's never too late to start new traditions," she says gently. "Especially around Christmas."

Her words strike a chord in me, stirring up memories of Christmases past–before the divorce, before life got so complicated. I used to love this time of year, I realize with a pang. When did I stop letting myself enjoy it?

We reach the stage area, where a group of middle school students are tuning their instruments. Leena's eyes are wide with wonder as she watches them prepare. This is her dream to be one of these kids who march across the stage with confidence. I pray she'll get there and doesn't give up.

Gabby leads us to a row of chairs right in front of the stage. As we sit down, I can't help but notice how natural Gabby is with Leena and how easily she puts both of us at ease.

"I have to go up. Let me know what you think, okay?" she asks Leena.

Leena folds her hands in her lap and sits taller. "Okay."

I watch as Gabby greets each student by name, offering words of encouragement and adjusting bow ties or hair ribbons with a motherly touch. There's a genuine warmth to her interactions that I find myself envying. How does she do it? How does she connect so easily with everyone around her?

The lights dim, and a hush falls over the crowd as the first notes of "Silent Night" fill the air. Leena leans against me, her small hand slipping into mine. She closes her eyes as if feeling the music inside of her instead of just hearing it. I marvel at this glimpse into the person my daughter is becoming.

As the music washes over us, I feel the stress of work, the constant worry about being a good enough father–it all fades into the background, replaced by the simple joy of being present in this moment.

I glance down at Leena, her face glowing with delight as she watches the performance. Then, almost involuntarily, my gaze shifts to Gabby. She's completely engrossed in the music, her eyes shining with pride for her students. As if sensing my gaze, she turns slightly, catching my eye.

For a brief moment, we share a smile, and I feel a warmth spread through my chest that has nothing to do with the stuffy gymnasium. It's a feeling I thought I'd buried long ago, a spark of possibility that thrills and terrifies me.

As the final notes of the song fade away, I find myself clapping enthusiastically along with the rest of the audience. Leena jumps to her feet, cheering for her older schoolmates.

"That was amazing!" she exclaims, turning to me. "Will I get to play like that someday?"

"Absolutely," I promise her. "You already have a wonderful start."

As the crowd begins to disperse, I realize with a start that we've been at the fair for over two hours. "We should probably head home," I say, surprised at the twinge of reluctance I feel.

As we make our way towards the exit, Leena chattering excitedly about the concert and all the crafts she saw, I can't help but glance back at the stage. Gabby is there, surrounded by her students, her face alight as she congratulates them on their performance.

For the briefest of moments, I allow myself to imagine what it might be like to be part of that joy, to open my heart to new possibilities. Then reality crashes back in–the responsibilities waiting for me at home, the fears that have kept me isolated for so long.

Still, as we step out into the crisp December air, snowflakes begin to fall around us, and I can't shake the feeling that something has shifted. A tiny crack has formed in the walls I've built around my heart, letting in a glimmer of hope I thought I'd lost long ago.

"Daddy," Leena says as we walk to the car, her small hand warm in mine, "can we come back to the fair tomorrow? Please?"

I feel a pang in my chest as I look down at her hopeful face. I feel like a jerk because I'm grateful the fair only lasts one day, and I have an excuse to tell her no, that doesn't have anything to do with my responsibilities at work.

"I'm sorry, princess," I say, trying to keep my voice gentle. "The fair only lasts one day."

Leena's face falls, her blue eyes filling with disappointment. "Oh. Okay."

As we climb into the car, I can feel the weight of her disappointment pressing down on me, and I'm tempted to stop at the store and buy a bag of cotton balls and pop cycle sticks so we can spend the rest of the day making ornaments. That's a pipe dream, though. I have a mountain of work to do, and if it's not done before midnight, I'll pay the price. I can't lose this job. It's the best thing we have going for us right now. I may not be able to be there all the time for Leena, but I have the financial means to make sure someone is there for her; we have a roof over our heads and food on our table. As she gets older, she'll understand and appreciate the sacrifices we've made. It's all for her.

"I know it's disappointing," I say as I start the car, "but sometimes we have to do things we don't want to do. I'll be at your concert in a couple of days."

"I know," she kicks the back of the passenger seat.

"You'll thank me one day when you see all the opportunities you have because of my hard work." I smile at her. "You can travel, go to college, have a big wedding. It'll be a great life."

She nods but turns to stare out the window.

As we drive home through the gently falling snow, the car is quieter than before. I try to ignore the gnawing feeling in my gut, focusing instead on the work waiting for me at home and switching on the part of my brain that works through the angles and comes up with the best argument to win a case.

This is the right decision, I tell myself. It has to be.

Unbidden, the image of Gabby's warm smile and kind eyes comes to mind. For a brief moment, I allow myself to wonder what might have happened if I'd invited her out for some cocoa. But then I push the thought away. There's no room for what-ifs in our life. We have to focus on what's practical and what's necessary.

This is for the best, I think, as we head inside. One day, Leena will understand. One day, I'll be able to slow down. Though I doubt I'll ever feel safe enough to trust someone with my heart again. That day will never come.

Two

TYLER

I slip into a folding chair near the back of the auditorium. Everywhere I look, twinkling lights and children's artwork are on display.

I shift uncomfortably, my suit jacket feeling suddenly too formal amidst the sea of festive sweaters and Santa hats. The weight of my phone in my pocket is a constant reminder of the mountain of work I've left behind to be here. A twinge of guilt nags at me; I shouldn't be here. There are briefs to review and clients to call.

The rustle of programs and murmur of proud parents fade as my mind drifts back to the office. I can almost hear Sandra, my assistant, fielding calls with increasing exasperation. "Mr. Olsen is unavailable at the moment," she'd be saying, her tone growing tighter with each repetition. My boss's disapproving frown flashes in my mind's eye. Taking time off during the day, especially this close to the holidays when everyone's trying to wrap up their affairs? It's career suicide.

A small hand tugs at my sleeve, jolting me from my reverie. "Daddy!" Leena's smile is so big it lights up my depressing thoughts. "You made it." She's wearing a red velvet dress with white tights and a white bow in her hair. I bought the outfit online a couple of weeks ago and surprised her this morning. She loved it. I'm grateful I can provide those little touches to make her life magical.

I force a smile, pushing aside thoughts of the office. "I wouldn't miss it," I tell her, even though I considered doing just that.

For a moment, I'm struck by how much she looks like her mother–the same golden curls, the same enthusiasm. How could she not want to be a part of Leena's life? Maybe I wasn't the best husband, but Leena didn't deserve to be left behind.

"Ladies and gentlemen," a voice booms over the PA system, "please take your seats. The Benton Falls Elementary School Holiday Concert is about to begin!"

Leena darts off. There's a flurry of movement as parents scramble to find their seats, and children file onto the risers or sit in seats behind music stands made for grownups. I crane my neck, searching for Leena among the sea of small faces to make sure she made it to her spot. She takes her seat and smooths out her dress.

The first notes of "Jingle Bells" ring out, slightly off-key but brimming with holiday spirit. I try to focus on the performance, but my mind keeps drifting. The Johnson case files are probably buried under a stack of holiday cards on my desk. Sandra will need them. I send her a text. And what about the deposition prep for next week? I should be reviewing testimonies. Maybe I can pull it up on my phone...

My phone vibrates. I glance around, seeing nothing but rapt faces illuminated by the soft glow of Christmas lights. Surely, no one would notice if I just checked quickly.

I slip out of my seat, wincing as the metal chair scrapes against the floor. A few heads turn, eyebrows raised, but I'm already halfway to the door.

In the relative quiet of the hallway, I answer the call. "Tyler Olsen speaking."

"Tyler, where the bells are you?" My boss's voice crackles through the speaker, sharp with irritation. "The Petersons are here for their meeting."

I curse under my breath. How could I have forgotten? "I'm so sorry, sir. There was a... family emergency. I'll be there as soon as I can."

"See that you are."

The line goes dead, leaving me with a knot of anxiety in my stomach. I run a hand through my hair, debating my next move. I could slip out now, maybe make it back to the office before the Petersons lose patience entirely.

"Excuse me, sir?" A gentle voice interrupts my internal struggle. I turn to see a beautiful woman with blonde hair and blue eyes the color of a clear winter's day, regarding me with a mixture of concern. "I'm Rose. The concert started. I'm sure whatever business you have can wait until after these children have their moment to shine."

"I'm sorry, who are you?" I ask gruffly.

"Rose." *Tap-tap-tappidy-tap.* "At your service."

Did she just tap dance? Weird. I shake my head. "I have an important meeting that I'm late for–."

"More important than Leena?" she asks, lifting an eyebrow.

Heat rises to my cheeks. "No. It's not... like that," I finish lamely. Shame washes over me as I realize how my behavior must look to others. What kind of father takes a business call during his daughter's Christmas concert?

"Maybe just a few more minutes then," Rose encourages me. She moves behind me and gives me a prod to get going.

"Are all the ushers this insistent?" I ask over my shoulder as I go through the door, letting the hallway light into the darkened auditorium and earning scowls from other parents.

I slink back to my seat. Leena's group is in the middle of "Silent Night" now, their small arms moving out of sync but the notes lining up.

"Isn't she darling," Rose whispers.

I jolt. I didn't notice her sit down next to me.

"She loves music," I muse. Leena's eyes are closed. She doesn't miss a note, and she sways with the beat, her face a picture of pure joy as she loses herself in the music.

Even as I see how much this means to her, I'm torn knowing what awaits me back at the office.

The concert stretches on endlessly–how many songs can these kids play? I check my watch compulsively, calculating how quickly I can make it back to the office if I leave the moment the last note fades. It's not that I don't want to be here for Leena—of course I do. But the pressure of work, of providing for her, of making sure she wants for nothing... it's crushing sometimes.

Finally, mercifully, the last song comes to an end. The gymnasium erupts in applause, proud parents leaping to their feet in a standing ovation. I go to move past Rose, but she puts a hand on my arm. "You can't leave without saying goodbye to her."

I stare down at this lady. She's right—but who is she to tell me what I can and can't do? And, darn it, I hate that she's right. Leena won't know how proud I am of her if I don't tell her, and I don't want her to be the only child without a parent to greet. I clap along mechanically, my mind racing ahead to the mountain of work awaiting me.

As the children file off the risers, the gymnasium becomes a chaotic swirl of reuniting families. I stand awkwardly to the side, watching as other parents sweep their children into warm embraces, voices raised in praise and celebration.

"Daddy!" Leena's voice cuts through the din, and suddenly, she's there, launching herself into my arms with the force of a tiny cannonball. "Did you see me? Did you hear me play?"

I hoist her up, breathing in the scent of her minty shampoo. The kind the hairdresser said would help her hair grow longer. I paid fifty-bucks for a bottle because Leena said she wanted her grow her hair out. She had no idea how much it cost, nor should she. I want her to know that she can have the world and that not having a mother to tuck her in at night doesn't mean she has to miss out on things in life. "I sure did. You were amazing up there."

Leena giggles. "I was so nervous, but then I saw you in the audience, and I wasn't scared anymore."

A lump forms in my throat. She saw me—even when I was distracted, even when I was halfway out the door, she saw me and drew strength from my presence. The realization is humbling and terrifying all at once. I can't do it. I can't be here and at work and all the things she needs me to do at once.

"I'm so proud of you, Leena," I manage, my voice thick with emotion.

Leena snuggles closer. "Can we get a Christmas tree? Please? Everyone else already has theirs!"

And just like that, my momentary peace shatters. The thought of trudging through a Christmas tree lot, wrestling with lights and ornaments, trying to create some semblance of holiday cheer in our too-quiet home... it's overwhelming. Memories of Christmases past crowd in—Sarah's laughter as we decorated together, the three of us a perfect little family unit. The betrayal of her absence hits me anew, as fresh as the day she walked out.

"I don't know," I hedge, setting Leena down gently. "Daddy's got a lot of work to do, and..."

Leena's face falls, disappointment clouding her bright eyes. "But it's Christmas," she says softly, her lower lip trembling. "We need a tree."

I don't even have words for this moment. She's a child and shouldn't carry any of this burden. I should put her on the bus and send her home to meet the babysitter and get back to the office. I know what I should do. So why do I want to throw all that out like last year's leftover stocking candy?

"Well, if it isn't my favorite glitter-covered lawyer," a warm, familiar voice chimes in, buying me some time.

I turn to see Gabby wearing a forest green dress that wraps around her middle and accentuates her curves. She has hips that I swear would fit perfectly in my hands—not that I would ever have the opportunity to test that theory.

Her chestnut curls are piled atop her head in a messy bun, a few stray tendrils framing her face. There's a softness about her, a genuine warmth that radiates outward.

"Ms. Robinson!" Leena exclaims, her earlier disappointment momentarily forgotten. She throws her arms around Gabby's lower half.

Gabby's smile widens as she crouches down to Leena's level. "You were absolutely wonderful up there. All that practice really paid off!"

Leena preens under the praise, and I feel a rush of gratitude towards Gabby for lifting my daughter's spirits so effortlessly. As she straightens up, her hazel eyes meet mine, twinkling with amusement.

"I see you managed to get all the glitter off, Tyler," she teases, her voice light. I enjoy how my name sounds on her lips. "I was half expecting to see you twinkling like a Christmas ornament."

Wait—she was thinking about seeing me again? That's ... unexpectedly awesome.

I feel a reluctant smile tugging at the corners of my mouth.

"Don't remind me," I groan, but there's no real annoyance behind it. "I think I'm still finding glitter in places I'd rather not mention."

Gabby laughs, the sound light and musical. "Well, you wore it well. Very festive."

There's something about her easy manner that always manages to crack me carefully and sets me at ease like I can just be myself around her. She's not my boss whom I have to impress or Leena, who I have to provide for and encourage. She's just Gabby but is also *Gabby*.

"Daddy," Leena pipes up, tugging on my sleeve. "We need a Christmas tree. Ms. Robinson, tell him we need a tree!"

Gabby's eyes widened slightly, and I could see her weighing her words carefully. We've had enough interactions for her to understand some of the complexities of our situation–the absent mother, my demanding job, the struggle to balance it all.

"Well," she says gently, "I haven't gotten my tree yet either, so don't think you're behind. I'm sure your dad knows what's best for your family and will get one when the time is right."

I feel a rush of gratitude for her diplomatic response and mouth *thank you* over Leena's head. It would be so easy for her to side with Leena, to paint me as the Grinch stealing Christmas–even in a teasing way. Instead, she's giving me an out while still validating Leena's desire.

I look down at Leena's hopeful face and realize that I

don't want an out on her. I want to give my daughter the Christmas she deserves. What did that woman say earlier? What's more important than Leena? Nothing. The Peterson is already angry, I'm already on my boss's Naughty List, and I'm going to have to give Sandra a day at the spa to make up for this, but I'm going to play hookey for an afternoon and buy my daughter a Christmas tree.

"You know what?" I hear myself saying the words, escaping before I can stop them. "I think the tree farm is open right now."

Leena squeals with delight, throwing her arms around my waist. "Thank you, Daddy! This is going to be the best Christmas ever!"

Over Leena's head, I catch Gabby's eye. She gives me a soft smile and a small nod as if to say, "You're doing the right thing." For a moment, I allow myself to bask in the warmth of her approval, in the joy radiating from my daughter.

I glance around for Rose to see if she saw this, too. She's not far away, giving a distraught child a tissue and a comforting pat on the back. The little boy's mom rushes over, expressing her gratitude that Rose found her son in this crowd. She seems to pay attention to details. I wonder where she's from. I haven't seen her around before.

"Well," Gabby says, drawing my attention back to her. "Maybe I'll follow your example and pick up my own tree this afternoon. Leena, remember to practice your solo, okay?"

Leena nods enthusiastically. "I'm going to practice every day!"

As Gabby turns to leave, she pauses, her eyes meeting mine once more. I feel all warm and gooey inside, and I find myself leaning towards her. "If you need any help with holiday stuff–decorating, baking, whatever–don't hesitate to ask. I know it can be overwhelming, especially when you're doing it alone," she says softly,

For a moment, I'm tempted to accept her offer. The thought of having someone to bring some lightness and laughter into our home... it's painfully appealing. But the walls I've built around my heart are high and thick, fortified by years of hurt and disappointment.

"Thanks," I manage, my voice gruffer than I intended. "We'll manage."

If Gabby is hurt by my brusque response, she doesn't show it. She simply nods, her smile never faltering. "Of course. Have fun, you two!"

As we make our way to the parking lot, Leena chattering excitedly about ornaments and candy canes, I can't help but glance back. Gabby is still standing there, watching us go with an expression I can't quite decipher. For a fleeting moment, I allow myself to imagine what it might be like to let her in. The image is too good to be true. I've seen both sides of this arrangement. At first, it's all flirting and kissing and bliss–but it can quickly turn to resentment and loneliness.

I can't open myself up like that again; I can't risk letting someone else in only to have them walk away. It's better this way, safer for both Leena and me.

Leena buckles in, her excitement palpable in the small space. As I slide into the driver's seat, I catch a glimpse of her in the rearview mirror. Her face is aglow with the magic of the season, eyes sparkling with anticipation.

I shoot off a text to Sandra asking her to cover my afternoon because of a family emergency. At least my story is the same across the board. I didn't think Christmas trees were emergencies, but there's more at stake here than a pine tree.

As we pull out of the school parking lot, Leena's voice pipes up from the backseat. "Daddy? Can we get hot chocolate while we look for our tree?"

I smile, surprising myself with how genuine it feels. Being able to say yes is a wonderful feeling. "Sure thing. Hot chocolate it is."

Our little Christmas adventure has begun.

Three

ROSE

My tap shoes, usually a source of joy and rhythm, now feel oddly heavy on my feet as I tread carefully across the snow-dusted ground of the Christmas tree farm.

I spot Tyler and Leena a few rows away, their figures silhouetted against the twinkling lights strung between the trees. It gets dark early here, and I'm still adjusting to the lack of light. In heaven, there's always light. It's wonderful. I can't quite adjust to the darkness, and I trip over extension cords that crisscross the ground to light up trees.

Tyler is a good man. I have seen his struggles today—every day, really. I want to help him, want to lift his burden. He has to do it, though. I can't do it for him—which is terribly frustrating.

My heart swells with affection for this man who carries the weight of the world on his shoulders. Leena is right there with him in my heart. She's the key to unlocking his heart, and she doesn't even know the influence she has in his life. She's just herself–hopeful and open. I'm so grateful he chose to take her Christmas tree hunting. It was a big step for him.

As I draw closer, I can sense Tyler's love for Leena. It radiates like a beacon, but it's tangled with threads of fear, insecurity, and a deep-seated belief that he must face every challenge alone. Humans are a beautiful, messy tapestry of conflicting desires and fears. It doesn't have to be that way, but somehow, it always seems to turn out like that for them.

"Daddy, look at this one." Leena's excited voice cuts through the chatter of the crowd. She's pointing to a tree that's at least three times her height, her blue eyes wide with wonder. "It's perfect!"

Leena speaks in absolutes. She's either extremely happy or sad or disappointed or hopeful. You can hear her feelings in her tone, like the bells on Christmas Eve.

Tyler chuckles, a rare sound indeed. "I think that might be a bit too big for our living room. How about we look for something a little smaller?"

I watch as Leena's face falls for a moment before brightening again. Her resilience is astounding, a quality I've come to admire in my short time observing her. "Okay. Can we get hot chocolate while we look? I'm cold all the way to my belly."

As Tyler nods, his eyes scanning the crowd for the concession stand, I sense a familiar presence nearby. I turn to see Gabby, the orchestra teacher, browsing for a tree. Her chestnut curls are tucked under a festive red hat, and her warm smile seems to light up the entire lot.

I can't help but smile as I watch her. There's something about Gabby that reminds me of the purest souls in heaven–a genuine kindness that radiates from within.

I look from Gabby to Tyler and then back again. Hmm. There's a thought about these two that wants to wiggle loose. I close my eyes for a moment, reaching out to gauge her emotions and see if I'm off my rocker. Some angels easily connect to people and just know what's going on inside of them. I have to work a little harder for it, but that's the way I was made, and I'm okay with that.

A swirl of Gabby's feelings washes over me–excitement for the holiday season, joy in helping others, and... nervousness? I focus more intently and realize her nerves come because Tyler is here. There's a longing there, a desire to approach him, but something's holding her back.

I smile to myself. It seems Gabby might need a little angelic intervention, too.

I set my plan in motion. As Leena skips ahead towards the hot chocolate stand, she's going to trot right past Gabby. Well, if that isn't a sign, I don't know what it is. I give her exuberant steps a subtle nudge. She stumbles, heading for a tree. Before Tyler can react, Gabby throws out her arm and steadys Leena.

"Whoa there, careful!" Gabby says, laughing as they both twirl because of the impact. "Are you okay?"

Leena nods, her eyes wide. "I tripped."

"You did. But I caught you." Gabby gives Leena a loving squeeze before letting her go.

Tyler rushes over, his face a mask of concern that quickly shifts to recognition. "Thank you. I couldn't catch up to her in time."

I watch intently as their eyes meet. For a moment, just a fleeting second, I see a spark of something in Tyler's gaze. A crack in his carefully constructed walls, a glimpse of the man he used to be before heartbreak, hardened his heart. As quickly as it appears, it's gone. Tyler's expression shutters, his defenses slamming back into place. "We appreciate your help. Come on, Leena, let's get that hot chocolate."

I sigh, tapping my foot in frustration. It's one step forward, two steps back with this guy. But I'm not deterred. If anything, this brief moment has shown me that there's still hope for Tyler. He just needs a few more nudges in the right direction. I rub my palms together.

Tyler and Leena head towards the concession stand, and Gabby's shoulders slump slightly. She watches them go, a wistful expression on her face. I'm still connected to her and I can feel her disappointment, her desire to connect with Tyler warring with her fear of rejection.

I make my way over to her. To human eyes, I look like any other Christmas shopper—just a friendly face in a festive sweater.

"Excuse me," I say, getting her attention. "I couldn't help but notice how quick you were to help that little girl. Are you a teacher?"

Gabby turns to me, her smile returning despite the lingering sadness in her eyes. "Yes, I am. I teach music."

"That's wonderful," I reply, genuine admiration in my voice. "Music is such a gift, especially during the holidays. Are you involved in any Christmas concerts?"

Her face lights up at the question, and I can feel her passion for music and teaching children radiating from her. "Actually, yes. I'll be volunteering at Santa's Workshop, helping with the children's choir and some of the musical activities."

"I know all about Santa's Workshop," I tell her. It's not a lie. I read up on it on a flier this afternoon at the concert while I watched the door to block Tyler from leaving. I reach into my pocket, producing a flyer for the Santa's Workshop event. It's a bit of angelic help–the flyer wasn't there a moment ago, but now it exists as surely as the trees around us.

"It's perfect that you happen to be here at this very moment," I exclaimed, handing her the flyer. "I was just about to give this to that gentleman and his daughter. Perhaps you could tell them more about it? I'm sure a little girl like that would love Santa's Workshop."

Gabby hesitates, her earlier nervousness returning. "Oh, I don't know... Mr. Olsen seems pretty busy. I wouldn't want to bother him."

I give her an encouraging smile. "I'm sure he'd appreciate the information, and if he chooses not to go, well, that's up to him. If we don't ask, we'll never know."

With a gentle nudge, I guide Gabby toward Tyler and Leena, who are just returning with their hot chocolates.

As we approach, I can feel Gabby's heart racing, her palms growing sweaty despite the winter chill.

"Tyler," I call out, my voice carrying just enough to catch his attention. "I hope I'm not interrupting, but I wanted to make sure you knew about the Santa's Workshop event. This lovely lady was just telling me all about it."

Tyler turns, his expression guarded but polite. "You?" His forehead wrinkles. He looks around as if wondering where I came from. I laugh to myself because he's looking every which way but up. "Do you work here?"

"I work wherever I'm needed," I reply with a smile. I elbow Gabby.

Gabby steps forward, her voice slightly shaky but growing in confidence as she speaks. "Santa's Workshop is a long-standing tradition in Benton Falls. There will be all sorts of activities for children–games, music, and even a chance to meet Santa. I thought... well, I thought Leena might enjoy it."

Leena's eyes light up at the mention of Santa. "Can we go, Daddy? Please? I didn't get to see Santa at the craft fair."

I watch Tyler closely, tuning into him. On one hand, I can feel his desire to make Leena happy, to give her the Christmas experience every child deserves. On the other, there's that ever-present fear of opening up, of allowing anyone–even his daughter, I realize with a start–too close to his heart. Oh, my goodness. No wonder this is such a dire case. My hand flies to my heart. There is no time to lose.

"I don't know, sweetheart," Tyler hedges.

"It's such a wonderful event," I interject, unable to keep silent. "Maybe you could even volunteer together?" I motion between the two of them. "It would be a great way to get into the Christmas spirit."

Gabby flushes at my suggestion, her gaze darting between Tyler and the ground. "Oh, well, I'll already be there volunteering. But there's always room for more help if you're interested, Mr. Olsen."

I can sense Tyler's defenses rising again, his body language becoming more closed off. But before he can respond, Leena tugs on his sleeve.

"Please, Daddy? It sounds so fun. And we could help Ms. Robinson."

For a moment, Tyler's expression softens as he looks at his daughter's pleading face. I hold my breath, hoping that this might be the breakthrough we need.

But then his phone buzzes in his pocket, and just like that, the moment is gone. "We'll think about it," he says, his tone making it clear that it's unlikely to happen. "I do need to log a certain number of volunteer hours before the end of the year for the firm. Thank you for the information. Leena, say goodbye. We need to finish picking out our tree." They move deeper into the tree farm.

"No problem." Gabby hurries away, and my heart sinks in for her. She really put herself out there, and Tyler hurt her feelings. Goodness, how did he not see the way she looked at him like he'd hung the moon?

As they walk away, Leena waving goodbye over her shoulder, I can't help but feel a mix of disappointment and determination. It wasn't the smooth intervention I had hoped for, but I've planted a seed. Now, I just need to nurture it and hope it grows.

I hurry after Gabby, who's fingering a tree branch with a wistful expression. "Don't give up," I tell her softly. "Sometimes, the most guarded hearts are the ones most in need of kindness."

She looks at me, surprise evident in her eyes. "I... thank you. I don't know why I care so much. He's just... there's something about him. And Leena is such a sweet girl."

I smile, feeling a surge of hope. "Trust your instincts. And keep an eye out at Santa's Workshop. You never know who might show up."

As I walk away, leaving Gabby to ponder my words, I can't help but feel a renewed sense of purpose. If I had to report back on my progress right now, I'd say I'm failing. But final grades aren't out yet. I have until Christmas Eve to help Tyler open his heart to the true meaning of family and love.

I look up at the star-studded sky, tapping out a quiet rhythm with my shoes. "Give me strength," I whisper to the heavens.

With a smile and a final tap of my foot, I disappear into the night, ready to plan my next move in this delicate dance of human hearts and heavenly intervention.

Four

TYLER

Fluorescent lights buzz overhead in my home office, casting a harsh glow on the stack of legal briefs sprawled across my desk. I rub my eyes, feeling the strain of hours spent poring over case files and client testimonies in an effort to make up the time I missed this week. The clock on the wall ticks relentlessly, a constant reminder of deadlines looming and billable hours slipping away. I got up at three in the morning to get back to it. My boss was not happy with me for rescheduling the Peterson meeting and I have to show him that I'm dedicated to this job.

As soon as I logged on, I saw his icon appear. He's watching. Always watching.

Let him. I can handle this.

I'm so engrossed in the intricacies of a particularly complex case that I almost miss the soft knock on my door. Looking up, I see Leena's small face peering around the frame, her blue eyes wide with a mixture of excitement and hesitation.

"Daddy?" Her voice is barely above a whisper, as if she's afraid to disturb me.

"What is it, pumpkin?" I try to keep the frustration out of my voice, but I can hear the edge of impatience creeping in. It's 8:00 a.m. I was counting on her sleeping in until nine.

Leena takes a tentative step into the office, her hands clasped in front of her, holding a piece of paper. "Santa's Workshop is today."

I manage to keep my groan inside. Santa's Workshop. The words immediately bring Gabby and her heart-shaped face to mind. She's popped into my thoughts on several occasions over the last week. I even saw her at the grocery store with her friend, Olivia. The two of them chatted and laughed as they picked out vegetables. I don't know her friend all that well, except that she's the art teacher at the high school, so I didn't stop to say hello. Who am I kidding? I didn't stop because I *wanted* to talk to Gabby. A man has to protect himself from the wiles of a beautiful woman, and Gabby has them in spades.

I glance down at my plaid pajamas. "I don't think Santa wants to see me in my pajamas."

Leena giggles.

"Should we get dressed and go over?" Maybe if we get there early enough, we'll miss the crowds, and I can get back to work.

Leena's face lights up; her smile is as bright as the

Christmas lights we haven't put up yet. "Really? We can go now?"

I nod, forcing a smile even as my mind races through all that I'm leaving behind. "Really. Let's go see Santa."

I can already feel my boss's disapproval as I log off. His icon is the last thing to disappear on my screen–like an omen of the chewing out I'm going to get on Monday.

Leena and I dress quickly and eat breakfast, which tastes like cardboard.

The drive to the community building is a whirlwind of Leena's excited chatter and my own internal struggle. Part of me is already back at my office, worrying about the briefs left unfinished and the calls I'll have to return. But another part, a part I often ignore, is looking forward to this rare moment of connection with my daughter. I loved being there for her at the concert, of knowing that she drew strength from my presence.

Garlands of evergreen and twinkling lights frame the entrance to the community center, and a large sign proclaims "Santa's Workshop" in cheerful red and green letters. The sight of it all–so bright and full of holiday cheer–makes me acutely aware of how little effort I've put into creating the same atmosphere at home. We haven't decorated our tree yet. Once we got it through the door, Leena was satisfied, and I was more than happy to postpone the trip to the attic in favor of putting on a movie and doing paperwork.

Leena's bouncing with excitement as we make our way inside, and I can't help but think of that lady who keeps showing up at things and tap dancing. I never did ask her what she was doing in town. Maybe she's visiting her family and overeager to get to know people. I don't have the bandwidth to help her out, though.

The moment we step through the doors, we're enveloped in a cocoon of warmth and the rich, sweet scent of gingerbread from the gingerbread house contest that is running all month long. I glance that way, knowing Leena would love to look at the amateur section that's complete and maybe even watch some of the professionals as they work on their masterpieces. The air is filled with the sound of children's laughter and the soft strains of "Away in a Manger" playing in the background.

"Tyler! Leena! You made it."

I turn to see Rose approaching us with a bright smile.

"Speak of the devil," I mutter under my breath.

Rose is wearing a festive sweater adorned with tiny cymbals of all things that chime softly as she walks. She's an odd duck, this one, but likable.

"I'm so glad you came," she says, her eyes twinkling. "Leena, why don't we go find Ms. Robinson? I heard she's helping with the ornament-making station."

At the mention of Ms. Robinson, I feel an unexpected flutter in my stomach. I push it aside, reminding myself that I'm here for Leena, not to indulge in some crush I have on her teacher.

Rose leads us through the bustling workshop, past tables laden with gift-wrapping supplies and children eagerly creating holiday masterpieces. The entire space is a riot of color and activity, with volunteers in elf hats guiding kids through various Christmas-themed activities.

And then I see her.

Gabby.

My breath catches.

She's more beautiful than I remember.

Her curls are pulled back in a messy bun as she helps a group of children wrap socks for the hospital. The soft glow of the fairy lights strung above catches the golden highlights in her hair, and for a moment, I'm struck by how angelic she looks.

Gabby looks up, her hazel eyes meeting mine. Her smile widens, and I feel that flutter again, stronger this time because that smile was for me. Mine all mine. A part of me rises up and wants to claim more of her. I tell it to chill out.

"Tyler," she breathes my name. We stare at one another until a boy slams into the side of her to show her his lumpy sock project. She congratulates him on a job well done and then turns to me and Leena. "I'm so happy you could make it," she says, her voice warm and genuine. "Would you like to join us in wrapping gifts?"

Leena nods enthusiastically, already reaching for a pre-cut piece of wrapping paper.

Before I can respond, my phone buzzes. "I... I need to take this," I mutter, already backing away. "Leena, why don't you stay here with Ms. Robinson? I'll be right back."

I catch a flicker of disappointment in Gabby's eyes.

Man, that woman knows how to make me feel wanted. I don't even think she's trying.

I answered for the client, who didn't care that it's Saturday morning. I'm supposed to be available 24/7– that's what they pay the firm for, isn't it? As I delve into the familiar territory of legal jargon and strategy, I feel a sense of relief. This, at least, I know how to handle. Gabby, on the other hand, feels like new territory.

From the corner of my eye, I watch as Gabby guides Leena through the process of wrapping a pair of socks–a task that seems much easier than it actually is. My attempts in the past led to a decorative bag and tissue paper. Their heads are bent close together, Gabby's hands gently guiding Leena's as she applies a long piece of tape. The sound of Leena's laughter drifts over, punctuating the serious conversation I'm having about property disputes and zoning laws.

As I hang up the phone, I'm struck by the contrast. Here I am, discussing the minutiae of legal proceedings; while just a few feet away, my daughter is creating Christmas memories that will last a lifetime. The realization sits uncomfortably in my chest, a weight I can't quite shake off.

I make my way back to the table, where Leena is proudly holding up her finished package. It's a mess of tape and ribbon with no discernible shape, but the joy on her face is undeniable.

"Daddy, look what I did," she exclaims. "Ms. Robinson helped me. Isn't it pretty?"

I nod, forcing a smile. "It's beautiful, sweetheart."

Gabby looks up at me, her eyes searching mine. "It's wonderful that you could take the time to come today, Tyler. I know how busy you must be, especially at this time of year."

There's no judgment in her voice, only genuine appreciation, but I still feel a twinge of guilt. "Thanks," I manage to say.

"Well, Tyler," she says, my name sounding different–better somehow–in her melodious voice, "since you're here, why don't you join us? I'm about to move to the cookie decorating station, and I have it on good authority that there will be taste testing involved."

Before I can come up with an excuse, Leena tugs on my hand, her eyes pleading. "Please, Daddy? Can we decorate cookies together?"

I hesitate, my boss's icon floating before my mental eye. The thing is, I don't want to spend time with that guy. He's rude, demanding, and constantly makes me feel like I have to prove myself. But here, in this space, I'm wanted and enough just because I'm *Tyler*. That's a great feeling and one that I could get used to. I don't remember the last time I felt right with myself. It's been years. I want to settle in and draw from this well. "Alright," I concede. "But just for a little while."

As we make our way to the cookie station, I can't help but notice how Gabby lights up the room. She greets each child we pass by name. It's clear that she's in her element here.

The cookie decorating table is full of frosting, sprinkles, and candy decorations. Leena dives in with gusto while I stand back, unsure of where to begin. Gabby notices my hesitation and sidles up next to me, a conspiratorial grin on her face.

"The key," she says in a stage whisper, "is to approach it like a work of art; just let your creativity flow."

I can't help but chuckle. "I'm afraid my artistic talents are limited to doodling in the margins of legal pads."

Gabby's laugh is like music. "Well then, counselor, consider this your first lesson in cookie artistry. Here, try this."

She hands me a sugar cookie shaped like a Christmas tree and a piping bag filled with green frosting. As I fumble with the unfamiliar tool, Gabby's hand gently covers mine, guiding my movements. The warmth of her touch sends a jolt through me, and for a moment, I forget about work, about my fears, about everything except the feeling of her hand on mine and the sweet scent of sugar in the air.

"There," she says softly, stepping back. "Now you're getting it."

I look down at the cookie, surprised to see a somewhat recognizable Christmas tree taking shape. Leena peers over, her eyes wide with approval.

"Wow, Daddy, that looks great," she exclaims, reaching for a handful of sprinkles to add to my frosting.

As we continue decorating, I find myself relaxing, drawn into the simple joy of the activity. Each cookie has its own shape, and I like adding the base layer of frosting so Leena can add the sprinkles, etc. Gabby moves between us, offering suggestions and praise in equal measure. Her laughter mingles with Leena's, creating a melody that warms something long dormant inside me.

I feel like . . . me. The best me. The me that wanted a family and a daughter and days filled with cookies and laughter.

Before I know it, we've decorated a small army of cookies, each more colorful and chaotic than the last. Gabby holds up a tray of our creations, her eyes dancing with mischief.

"Now comes the best part," she announces. "The taste test!"

We each select a cookie, and on Gabby's count of three, take a bite. The sweetness explodes on my tongue, and I'm shocked that I can taste it. Really taste it. It's like I've been asleep for a long time, and I'm waking up. Leena giggles as frosting smears across her chin and even I can't help but laugh at the mess we've made of the table and ourselves. I have green frosting on my sleeve, and Leena has red fingerprints on her shirt.

As we finish our cookies, I catch Gabby looking at me, a soft smile playing at the corners of her mouth. There's something between us–understanding and maybe a hint of something more–that makes my heart skip a beat. For the first time in years, I feel a spark of possibility, a connection, and I don't want to smother it.

Until I realize that this moment is not my real life. It feels real–more real than anything I've experienced since the doctor laid Leena in my arms and told me I had a daughter.

But it's not. It's what happens when I forget that I'm a single dad with bills to pay.

I clear my throat, taking a step back, both physically and emotionally.

"We should probably move on to the next station," I say, my voice sounding strained even to my own ears. "Leena, why don't we go see what they're doing over at the card-making table?"

Gabby is all smiles. I don't know if she picked up on my retreat or if she's being positive for Leena's sake. "Of course. I need to head over there anyway to help set up. Leena, would you like to learn how to make a pop-up card?"

Leena nods enthusiastically, already racing towards the next table. I follow more slowly, watching as Gabby effortlessly transitions to her new role, patiently demonstrating the intricate folds and cuts needed to create three-dimensional Christmas trees and snowmen.

She seems to have an endless well of patience, offering encouragement and praise to even the most fumble-fingered attempts. Maybe that's why she doesn't get mad at me for falling into the holiday spirit and then out of it again just as quickly.

I'm so lost in thought that I barely notice when someone sidles up beside me. It's Rose again, her cymbal sweater announcing her presence before she speaks.

"She's quite something, isn't she?" Rose says, nodding towards Gabby.

I grunt noncommittally, not wanting to reveal the turmoil of emotions Gabby's presence stirs in me.

Rose, however, seems undeterred by my reticence. She looks me directly in the eye, and I squirm. "You know, Tyler, it's okay to let people in sometimes. Even strong, independent lawyers need a little help now and then."

"I appreciate the advice, but I'm not looking for... that. I'm here for Leena, that's all."

Rose's eyes twinkle knowingly. "Why don't you join them at the table? I bet Gabby would appreciate some adult company amidst all these little ones. Maybe you're not the only one who needs some help. It's not always about you."

I blink as her words hit home. Still, I want to argue. I'm a lawyer, after all. "Everything I do, I do for Leena. It's never about me."

Rose scoffs. "Keep telling yourself that."

"What do you base your statement on?" I put one hand on my hip in a very un–lawyerly–like stance.

"You'll figure it out one day–hopefully sooner rather than later. In the meantime, don't let that beautiful woman wonder if you're ever going to get close to her." She gives me a gentle push towards the card–making station. I stumble forward, finding myself face-to-face with Gabby once again.

"Perfect timing," she says, her smile brightening. "We could use an extra pair of hands. How are you with scissors?"

For the next hour, I'm immersed in a world of colorful paper, glue sticks, and glitter. I can't seem to escape the stuff this season. "I can't remember ever even noticing glitter before," I tell Gabby. "And now I wear it on a weekly basis." I brush some off my sleeve. It's no use; it's globbed onto the frosting, and it made friends.

Gabby laughs.

She moves around the table, offering guidance and praise, but she always seems to gravitate back to where Leena and I are working.

Olivia Sanchez, the art teacher, stops by the table and places a hand on Gabby's shoulder. She looks at the rest of us and asks, "Mind if I borrow her for a moment?"

One of the moms waves her off. "We're good for a few minutes."

I watch Gabby leave. She glances over her shoulder and catches me looking, and I drop my gaze on the table. I don't need to be watching her at all. I certainly don't need to blush because she caught me. I use a piece of cardstock to fan my face until I'm back to normal.

As we put the finishing touches on our cards, I overhear a conversation between two volunteers nearby. I don't know who they are—teachers, maybe?

One of them has enough of a baby bump that it's obvious she's pregnant. "Poor Ms. Robinson," she whispers. "It must be hard for her this time of year, being alone and all."

The other nods sympathetically. "I heard she doesn't have any family in town. Can you imagine spending Christmas by yourself?"

Their words hit me hard, and Rose's admonition that it's not always about me comes back with force. I look at Gabby, really look at her, as she and Olivia lift a fake tree and move it across the room. Decorations fall off and bounce away. She laughs as if this is no big deal. It probably isn't, but I can't help but think that my ex would have broken into tears and fits over it.

For the first time, I see a hint of loneliness that resonates with my own carefully hidden pain.

Before I can dwell on this revelation, Leena grabs my arm. "Can we make a card for Ms. Robinson?"

"I'm sure she gets plenty of cards," is my first response. She's a teacher, for heaven's sake–one the kids actually like. "She doesn't need one from me, but if you want to make one, you can." I look up and see Rose. She lifts an eyebrow at me, a silent dare to get out of my own situation and lift someone else's day.

I find myself glancing around the room with new eyes. How many others here feel as isolated as I do, even in the midst of all this festive cheer? The thought is sobering, and for the first time in a long while, I feel a genuine desire to reach outside of my little circle.

Leena is engrossed in her own creation, giving me a moment of privacy. With a deep breath, I select a piece of red cardstock and begin to fold it. I attach a large sticker on the front, feeling like a complete idiot. My mind races with what to say. There are so many options–so many meanings behind every word. I don't stumble in the courtroom, so why am I struggling here?

In the end, I keep it simple:

Gabby,

Thank you for bringing joy and music into Leena's life–and mine.

Merry Christmas,
Tyler

The alarm goes off on my phone. Leena sets her scissors down, and her shoulders slump. "Time to go?"

I hate that she knows that sound well enough to know it means the end of fun. "It is. Are you ready?"

She nods. As we prepare to leave, I find myself hesitating. Gabby is across the room, helping to redecorate the tree she just helped move. Leena tugs on my hand. "I left my coat by the cookies."

"Go ahead and grab it," I tell her. "I'll be right there."

With my heart pounding, I make my way over to Gabby. She looks up as I approach, a questioning smile on her face.

"Tyler? Is everything okay?"

I nod. My palms are sweating, and I resist the urge to wipe them off my pants. *Play it cool, man,* I tell myself. "Everything's fine. I just... I wanted to give you this." Her friend ducks away, a knowing smile on her face. I hold out the card, feeling oddly vulnerable. "Thank you for everything you do for Leena and for all the kids. It... it means a lot."

Gabby takes the card, her fingers brushing mine in the process. The contact sends a jolt through me, and for a moment, I'm tempted to reach out and pull her to me. Just a hug. Friends hug, don't they? I can definitely say we're friends–we survived glitter disasters and frosting flops. I just can't seem to cross that line, though.

"Tyler, I... thank you," she says softly, her voice filled with genuine emotion. "This is so thoughtful of you."

She opens the card, her eyes scanning the simple message inside. When she looks back up at me, there's a warmth in her gaze that makes my breath catch.

She says, reaching out to touch my arm gently. "Thank you."

For a moment, we stand there, connected by that simple touch and the unspoken understanding that passes between us. I feel the walls around my heart trembling, threatening to crumble under the weight of her kindness and the unexpected connection in the moment.

"I found my coat," Leena says proudly as she approaches.

I clear my throat but don't move out of Gabby's grasp. Instead, I put my hand over hers. She looks down at the place where we connect and then back up at me, a silent question in her eyes.

"I... we should go," I mumble.

Gabby nods, her smile tinged with a hint of disappointment that makes my heart ache. "Of course. Thank you again, Tyler. For the card and for coming today. It really does make a difference."

As I turn to go, I find myself wanting to say more, to bridge the gap that I've so carefully maintained. "Merry Christmas, Gabby." The words don't even begin to cover what I'm feeling, but they seem to do the trick.

"Merry Christmas, Tyler," she replies, her voice soft and warm like a cozy blanket on a cold winter's night. I get the feeling that I'm safe with her in a way I haven't known before.

The joy of the day, the warmth of Gabby's presence,

and the persistent whisper of my own insecurities all vie for attention. For the first time in longer than I can remember, I've spent an entire morning without once checking my phone or worrying about work. We step outside, and I hold the door for an elderly gentleman as he slowly hobbles in.

"Did you have fun?" I ask Leena as we make our way to the car.

She nods enthusiastically, her cheeks rosy from excitement and sugar. "It was the best day ever."

"That's quite the endorsement," I tease her.

The drive home is filled with Leena's excited chatter about everything we did and saw. I listen with half an ear, my mind replaying every interaction with Gabby. I can still feel her hand on mine as we decorate cookies and the softness of her sweater when she brushed up against me.

As we pull into our driveway, I'm struck by how dark and uninviting our house looks compared to the festive warmth of Santa's Workshop. The bare windows and undecorated porch stand in stark contrast to the cheerfully decorated homes of our neighbors.

"Daddy?" Leena's voice is small and hesitant. "Can we put up our Christmas lights this year?"

I look at her in the rearview mirror, seeing the hope and uncertainty in her eyes. It's the same look she had when she reminded me about Santa's Workshop, the look that says she's bracing herself for disappointment but can't quite extinguish the spark of childish optimism.

In that moment, I see myself through her eyes–the constantly busy father, always with one foot out the door, promising "later" and "soon" but rarely delivering. The realization hits me, and I make a decision that surprises even myself.

"I think that's a great idea."

Leena's face lights up, her smile brighter than any Christmas light. "Really? You promise?"

I nod, feeling a weight lift from my shoulders even as a new one settles in its place–the weight of responsibility, of keeping this promise no matter what. "I promise, Leena. This year, we'll do Christmas right."

We go inside, and Leena skips ahead to her room with her bag of cookies and cards. For a moment, I allow myself to picture Gabby here with us, her warm presence filling the empty spaces in our home and in our hearts. The image is so vivid, so achingly appealing, that it takes my breath away.

I can't keep living like this. I know that now. I've seen the warmth on the other side of my cold detachment, and I have to make a change. I make a silent vow that I will do Christmas better. I will open my heart to the season and let Christ into my life this month. It's a risk. It means reevaluating some things and making changes. I feel ready for it, though. I don't want to go back to the curmudgeon I was yesterday. I want to live in this Season of Peace. For however long I can.

Five

TYLER

The heavy wooden door of my boss's office closes behind me with a soft thud, but the sound echoes in my mind like a gavel sealing my fate. So much for a Season of Peace. I played, and I paid for it.

The plush hallway carpet muffles my footsteps as I make my way back to my office, each step feeling heavier than the last. The scent of pine-scented cleaner lingers in the air, a stark reminder of the holiday season I dove into over the weekend only to have to jump back out of when Monday came.

"Tyler," my boss's words replay in my head, "I need to see more commitment from you. We're considering candidates for a partner, and right now, you're not at the top of the list."

I sink into the leather chair behind my desk, the familiar creak a small comfort in the face of potential failure. My eyes drift to the framed photograph on my desk–Leena's gap-toothed smile beaming at me, her blue eyes twinkling with a joy I can barely remember feeling myself. I pick up the frame, my thumb tracing the edge of her face. If I lose my job, then Leena won't have violin lessons, and the joy she finds in playing will be taken from her.

"I won't let you down," I whisper to the photograph.

Even as I say the words, a nagging doubt creeps in. Am I really doing what's best for Leena? Or am I using her as an excuse to bury myself in work, to avoid facing the emptiness that's been gnawing at me since Sarah left?

It's been years, but the pain of her betrayal still feels fresh some days. I can still hear her words, sharp and cutting: "I need more than this. I need to feel alive and free."

I set Leena's photo down, my gaze drifting to the window. Outside, snow falls gently, blanketing the street in a pristine white cover. The site should be peaceful, but all I can think about is how much harder it will be to get Leena from her after-school program in this weather.

A glance at my watch sends a jolt of panic through me. I'm already running late. I hastily gathered my briefcase and coat, my mind racing with calculations of how many hours I'll need to log from home tonight to make up for leaving before the boss.

As I rush past the reception desk, Mrs. Benson, the office receptionist, gives me a knowing look over her reading glasses. Her silver hair is perfectly coiffed as always, and there's a warmth in her eyes that makes me pause despite my hurry.

"Heading out to pick up Leena?" she asks, her voice gentle.

I nod. "Yes, I'm already running late," I admit, my hand on the door.

Something in her expression makes me hesitate, and Rose's advice comes to me again. "Mrs. Benson," I find myself asking, "do you have any plans for the holidays?"

Her face lights up, years seeming to melt away as she smiles. "My son and his family are coming to visit. We'll have a full house–Christmas music, baking cookies, the whole works."

As she describes her plans, I feel a pang of envy mixed with relief. Envy for the warmth and connection she'll experience, relief that this kind woman won't be alone during the festive season.

"That sounds wonderful," I say, meaning it despite the ache in my chest. "I hope you have a great time."

Her smile softens, and for a moment, I think she might say something more. But she just nods, waving me off. "You better get going. Don't want to keep Leena waiting."

The drive to Leena's after–school program is a blur of windshield wipers and holiday traffic. By the time I pull up to the community center, the sky has darkened to a deep indigo, and the streetlights cast a warm glow on the freshly fallen snow.

My heart sinks as I realize I'm the last car to make it to pick up. Leena and Gabby sit together on a bench outside the building. Leena's golden curls peek out from under a woolen hat, and she's animatedly talking to

Gabby, whose chestnut hair cascades over her shoulders in gentle waves.

As I approach, I'm already crafting an apology. "I'm so sorry I'm late," I begin, the words tumbling out in a rush. "There was a meeting, and then the snow..."

Gabby looks up, her hazel eyes warm and understanding. "Don't worry about it, Tyler," she says, her voice as melodious as ever. "Leena and I were just having a nice chat about her favorite Christmas carols."

Leena jumps up, wrapping her arms around my waist. "Ms. Robinson knows all the words to *Frosty the Snowman*. Even the part about the traffic cop."

I can't help but smile at her enthusiasm.

Gabby stands, brushing snow from her coat. "You know," she says, a hint of hesitation in her voice, "I was just about to head home and make some dinner. Why don't you two join me? I always make too much for just myself, anyway."

The offer catches me off guard. Part of me–a larger part than I care to admit–wants to accept immediately. The thought of a home-cooked meal and warm company is painfully appealing. But the responsible part of my brain kicks in, reminding me of the mountain of work waiting at home.

"That's very kind of you," I start, "but I really should get home. I have some work to catch up on and–"

"Daddy," Leena interrupts, her blue eyes wide and pleading, "can we please go?"

I hesitate, torn between my responsibilities and the

tempting offer before me. Leena, ever perceptive, pipes up again.

"It'll be faster than your cooking, Daddy. Remember when you tried to make spaghetti, and the smoke alarm went off?"

I feel my cheeks flush, but Gabby's gentle laughter eases the sting. "Well," I say, surprising myself, "when you put it that way, how can I refuse? But we'll eat and run–I don't want to impose."

Gabby's smile broadens, lighting up her entire face. "It's no imposition at all."

The drive to Gabby's house is short. Her home is a cozy bungalow on a quiet street, its porch adorned with twinkling lights and a festive wreath. As we step inside, the aroma of simmering herbs and spices envelops us, making my mouth water.

"Make yourselves at home," Gabby says, hanging up her coat. "Dinner should be ready in about ten minutes."

As Leena explores the living room, exclaiming over Gabby's collection of musical instruments, I find myself drawn to the kitchen. Gabby moves with easy grace, stirring the crockpot and pulling plates from the cupboards.

"Can I help with anything?" I ask, feeling oddly out of place in this warm, lived–in space.

Gabby smiles over her shoulder. "You could set the table if you'd like. Placemats are in that drawer there."

As we work side by side, a comfortable silence falls between us. The clink of plates and the soft bubbling of the crockpot create a domestic symphony that stirs something inside of me. I allow myself to imagine what it would be like to have this every day—coming home to a warm house, the scent of dinner cooking, Leena's laughter echoing through the rooms.

The longing that sweeps through me is so intense it's almost painful. I clear my throat, pushing the dangerous thoughts aside. "This smells amazing," I say, grasping for something safe to talk about.

Gabby's eyes crinkle at the corners as she smiles. "It's a simple beef stew. My grandmother's recipe—perfect for cold nights like this."

As we settle around the table, Leena chattering excitedly about her day, I'm struck by how natural this feels. Gabby listens intently to Leena's stories, asking questions and laughing at her jokes. The stew is delicious, rich, and hearty, warming me from the inside out.

"So, Tyler," Gabby says during a lull in the conversation, "Leena tells me you're working on a big case. That must be exciting."

I nod, swallowing a mouthful of stew. I'm always working on a case. Leena probably thinks it's the same one I started three years ago. "We're representing a small business owner in a dispute with a larger corporation. It's David versus Goliath, in a way."

Gabby leans forward, her interest seeming genuine. "That sounds fascinating. I'd love to hear more if you're allowed to disclose more that is."

The rest of the meal passes in a blur of conversation and laughter. Before I know it, we're clearing the table, and I realize with a start that nearly two hours have passed.

"We should get going," I say reluctantly, glancing at my watch. "I still have some work to finish up tonight."

Gabby nods, but there's disappointment in her eyes. "Of course. I'm glad you could come."

As we gather our coats, Leena yawns widely, the excitement of the evening catching up with her. Gabby kneels down, helping her button up her coat.

"Thank you for coming over, Leena," she says warmly. "I had a wonderful time."

Leena throws her arms around Gabby's neck in a spontaneous hug. "Can we come again?"

I find myself nodding before I can think better of it. "If Ms. Robinson doesn't mind."

Gabby's smile is radiant as she stands. "I'd like that very much."

As we step out into the cold night air, snowflakes swirling gently around us, I'm struck by a sense of possibility I haven't felt in years. The warmth of the evening lingers, a stark contrast to the chill that usually settles over me as I face another night of work ahead.

"Goodnight, Tyler," Gabby says softly. "Drive safe."

"Goodnight, Gabby," I reply, her name feeling familiar and new all at once on my tongue. "And thank you. For everything."

As we drive home, Leena is already half asleep in the backseat. I can't shake the image of Gabby standing in the doorway, illuminated by the warm light from within. The work waiting for me at home suddenly seems less daunting. As I tuck Leena into bed, her sleepy voice murmurs, "I like Ms. Robinson, Daddy. She makes you smile."

I pause, struck by the simple truth of her observation. "She does, doesn't she?" I whisper, more to myself than to Leena.

As I settle in at my desk, the familiar glow of my laptop screen illuminating the dark room, I find my thoughts drifting away from legal briefs and back to the warmth of Gabby's kitchen.

With a renewed sense of purpose, I turn to my work, the memory of laughter and a shared meal fueling me through the long night ahead. Tomorrow is another day, and for once, I'm looking forward to what it might bring.

Six

ROSE

The soft glow of the Heavenly Guidance Office envelops me as I stand near my desk. The air is filled with a subtle fragrance of blooming flowers, a scent that never fails to soothe even the most anxious of newly arrived souls. My fingers brush against the smooth surface of my desk, tracing the intricate patterns of the celestial map etched into its surface.

As I prepare for my next assignment, I can't help but let my thoughts drift back to Earth, to Tyler and his daughter Leena. I feel as though I'm coming across as heavy-handed, and Tyler is annoyed by my advice. I'm not sure how to get through to him otherwise–he's a bit of a tough nut to crack with his lawyerly, argumentative mind. The weight of my assignment sits heavily on my heart. I can't fathom Tyler alone every Christmas–and losing Leena will break him. I have to help him see that the path he's on will not take him to where he wants to go.

I'm not sure how to open his eyes fully.

I push those worries aside as I sense a new presence approaching.

A man steps into the office, his eyes wide with wonder and trepidation. He's tall and lean, with salt-and-pepper hair and kind brown eyes that speak of a lifetime of caring for others. I can sense the residual stress and fatigue from his earthly life clinging to him like a fading mist. It won't be there for long, though.

"Welcome," I say, as I gesture to the chair in front of my desk for him to sit in. "I'm Rose, your guidance counselor. Can you state your full name, please?"

The man clears his throat, his voice slightly shaky. "Dr. James Richardson. I... I'm not quite sure why I'm here."

I smile gently. As he settles in, I can feel the tension radiating from him in waves.

"It's perfectly normal to feel a bit lost at first, Dr. Richardson," I assure him. We don't use titles like Doctor in Heaven, but I think he will feel more situated if I address him as he wishes. "We're here to help you transition into your new... existence."

James nods, his fingers fidgeting with the hem of his white coat—a remnant of his earthly profession that he hasn't quite let go of yet. When he's ready, he'll transition to the white robes the rest of us wear. They're comfortable and airy, with a bit of majesty thrown in. I rather like them.

I lean forward, eyes meeting his. "Tell me, James, what did you do in your earthly life?"

"I was a pediatric surgeon," he says, a note of pride creeping into his voice. "Spent forty years saving children's lives."

I nod, admiring his dedication. "That's a noble calling, James." I flip through his thick fine. "You've touched so many lives."

He smiles, but it fades quickly. "So, what now? Do I... continue being a doctor here?"

I take a deep breath, knowing that my next words might be difficult for him to hear. "No. There's no sickness in heaven, James. However, I have a rather unique opportunity for you. How would you feel about taking on the role of celestial janitor in the Heavenly Mess Hall?"

James blinks, his mouth opening and closing a few times before he manages to speak. "I'm sorry, did you say janitor?"

I nod, keeping my expression warm and encouraging. "I know it might seem... unexpected. But we believe in giving souls the chance to explore new paths, to step outside their comfort zones."

James leans back in his chair, his brow furrowed. "But I'm a doctor. I've spent my entire life healing people. How can I just... give that up?"

My voice is gentle but firm. "James, think of this as an opportunity to heal in a different way. The Mess Hall is where newly arrived souls gather, where they find comfort and community. By maintaining order there, you'll be creating a welcoming environment for those who are still adjusting to their new existence."

I can see the conflict in his eyes, the struggle between clinging to his familiar identity and embracing this new adventure.

"Plus," I add with a wink, "I hear the manna is to die for. Pun intended."

A reluctant chuckle escapes James's lips, and I feel a small surge of triumph at getting through to him.

"I don't know," James says, his voice uncertain. "It's just so... different from everything I've known."

I nod sympathetically. "Change can be scary, even here. But think of it this way–you've spent your entire earthly life carrying the weight of life and death on your shoulders. Here, you have the chance to be free of that burden, to explore new aspects of yourself without the pressure."

James is quiet for a long moment, his eyes distant as he processes my words. I resist the urge to push further, knowing that this decision is his.

Finally, he takes a deep breath and meets my gaze. "Alright," he says, a hint of a smile tugging at his lips. "I'll give it a try. Who knows? Maybe I'll discover I have a hidden talent for mopping floors."

I beam at him. "I have a feeling you're going to bring a whole new level of care to the Mess Hall."

As I stand to shake his hand, a familiar presence enters the office. I turn to see Henry, his silver hair gleaming in the soft light. I sense the urgency in his demeanor and feel as though the clouds have disappeared under my feet.

"Rose," he says, his voice carrying a note of concern. "Might I have a word?"

I nod, turning back to James. "Dr. Richardson, why don't you head down to the Mess Hall? Timothy will be there to show you the ropes."

As James leaves, looking both nervous and excited, I brace myself for this conversation with my mentor. Things are not moving as quickly as I'd like with Tyler, and I'm at a loss as to how to push him without pushing him off the path.

"Rose," Henry begins, his blue eyes piercing mine. "How is your progress with Tyler Olsen?"

I take a deep breath, choosing my words carefully. "There's been some improvement," I say. "He's starting to soften; spend more time with Leena. Just the other day, they had dinner at Gabby's house–a real breakthrough, considering how closed off he's been."

Henry nods, but I can see the concern in his eyes. "That's a start, but time is running short, Rose. You know what's at stake here."

I swallow hard, feeling the weight of his words. "I know," I say softly. "If I can't guide Tyler towards embracing the spirit of family before midnight on Christmas Eve..."

"Not only will Tyler lose Leena forever, but you'll forfeit your chance to earn your wings for another thousand years," Henry finishes.

The reality of it hits me anew, and I feel a flutter of panic in my chest. I don't want to be a guidance counselor for another thousand years. I do like helping newly arrived angels, but I end up having the same three conversations over and over again. I need variety.

I glance down and realize that I haven't tapped so much as a pinkie toe since Henry walked in.

"I'm trying, Henry," I say, unable to keep the frustration out of my voice. "But Tyler... he's so guarded. Every time he takes a step forward, something pulls him back."

Henry places a comforting hand on my shoulder. "I know it's challenging. But you're learning too–about patience, perseverance, and the complexities of the human heart." Henry pauses, his expression softening. "Sometimes, no matter how hard we try, we can't change someone who isn't ready to change. But that doesn't mean your efforts are in vain. Every act of love and kindness ripples out into the universe, creating change in ways we can't always see."

With those words, he's gone, leaving me alone with my thoughts. As Henry's words sink in, I feel a profound connection with Tyler. Just as I've been challenged to take risks and trust in the divine plan, I'm now asking Tyler to trust in the possibility of love and connection, despite his past heartbreak.

I close my eyes, reaching out with my empathic abilities to sense Tyler's current emotional state. Even across the veil between heaven and Earth, I can feel the turmoil in his heart–the longing for connection warring with his fear of being hurt again.

"Oh, Tyler," I whisper to the empty office. "If only you could see how much love is waiting for you if you'd just open your heart."

It's almost time to return to Earth, anyway. I stand, smoothing down my celestial robes and taking a deep breath.

Time may be running short, but I'm not giving up. Tyler Olsen may be stubborn, but I've got heaven on my side and a pair of tap shoes ready to dance my way into his heart, if that's what it takes.

With a determined smile, I set off down the street, my feet tapping out a rhythm of hope on the snow-covered sidewalk.

Seven

TYLER

The aroma of freshly made pancakes and brewing coffee envelops me as I step into the bustling community center. I'm not sure how I ended up here. One moment, I was chatting up Gabby in the school parking lot as I picked up Leena and the next, we're in line for a pancake dinner. I may have mentioned it to Gabby as a way to gauge her interest in spending more time with Leena and me. But I'm still trying to catch up from how quickly we went from talking about the dinner to being in line for food.

The cheerful chatter and laughter of families fill the air, creating a festive atmosphere that's a balm to my haggard soul. I won the David and Goliath case, which earned me a hearty congratulations from my boss. It was quickly followed by a strong admonition to keep up the good work or else.

Despite the warmth and joy surrounding me, I can't shake the feeling of being slightly out of place. We look like a family. The thought sends an uncomfortable jolt through me. It's been so long since I've been part of a "family" in that sense that I'm not sure what to do with it. We aren't a family. Not like that.

We're also not on a real date. I mean, who takes their daughter with them on a date? I'm not sure what to call this evening, and that sets me on edge. I'm a man who likes to know the rules, all the players, their roles, and what is expected of them.

Leena bounces with excitement, her golden curls bobbing as she cranes her neck to catch a glimpse of Santa at the griddle. Gabby stands on Leena's other side. The sight of them together, so at ease and happy, only adds to the image of a family.

"Can we go watch?" Leena tugs on my hand, pointing towards the front of the room where Santa, in all his red-suited glory, is flipping pancakes with a flourish. She grabs Gabby's hand and pulls her, too.

I allow myself to be pulled along by my daughter's enthusiasm. As we make our way through the crowd, I can't help but notice the curious glances and whispers that seem to follow us. It's not like I'm well-known in town, but Gabby is a superstar.

We find a spot near the griddle, close enough to feel the warmth radiating from it and to smell the sweet scent of batter cooking. Santa's hearty laugh booms out as he shapes a pancake into what looks like a reindeer, much to the delight of the children gathered around.

"Ho Ho Ho! Who wants Rudolph?" Santa calls out, his eyes twinkling behind his spectacles.

Leena's hand shoots up, her face alight with joy. "Me, me!" she calls out, jumping up and down.

As Santa slides the reindeer-shaped pancake onto a plate and hands it to Leena.

"That's quite the pancake," Gabby says, her voice warm with amusement. "I think Rudolph's nose might be a little lopsided, though."

Leena giggles, carefully carrying her plate as we make our way to an empty table. "That's okay," she declares.

I snag two plates of regularly shaped pancakes and follow her.

As we settle into our seats, I slide a plate across to Gabby, who thanks me.

I can't help but notice how naturally Gabby interacts with Leena, helping her pour the syrup and cut her pancake into manageable bites. There's an ease to their relationship that I appreciate.

"Tyler?" Gabby's voice breaks through my thoughts. "Would you like some cocoa?"

I nod, grateful for the distraction. "That would be great, thanks."

As Gabby stands to get our drinks, I find my eyes following her, taking in the graceful way she moves through the crowd. She pauses to chat with a few people she knows, her laughter carrying back to our table.

"Daddy?" Leena's voice draws my attention back to her. "Do you think Ms. Robinson could help us decorate our tree? She said she knows how to make paper snowflakes," she says as if that overly qualifies Gabby for the job.

She comes back before I can answer Leena, and we all tuck in. The pancakes are good, and the hash browns on the side taste like pepper.

"Well, well, if it isn't the lovely Olsen family."

I choke on my hash browns. *Family* is a trigger word for me today.

I look up to see Rose standing beside our table. She grins at us in turn. "You three make such a beautiful picture." Her smile widens. "It's wonderful to see families coming together for the holidays."

"Oh, we're not–" I start to say, but Leena interrupts.

"Your shoes are so shiny!" She points to Rose's feet, where a pair of gleaming tap shoes peek out from beneath her wide-legged pants.

Rose's face lights up. "Why thank you, Leena! Do you like them?" She does a quick shuffle step, and Leena's face lights up at the sound. "They're tap shoes."

Leena nods enthusiastically. "They're so pretty."

"Are you part of the entertainment?" asks Gabby.

It's a good question. I see Rose everywhere, it seems, and she's always helping someone.

Rose shakes her head. "Tap dancing helps me think. Sometimes, when I'm trying to figure something out, I just start tapping away, and before I know it, the answer comes to me."

Leena's eyes widen with wonder. "Really? I want to see."

I'm about to intervene to explain that this isn't the time or place for a dance performance, but Rose is already moving to an open space near our table.

"Why not?" she says with a wink. "Dinner and a show, eh?"

Before I can protest, Rose launches into an impromptu tap dance routine. Her feet move in a blur of synchronized steps and rhythmic taps. People turn to watch, their faces lighting up with surprise and delight.

As I watch Rose dance, something shifts within me. The joy on her face, the abandon with which she moves—it's infectious.

Without thinking, I reach for Gabby's hand. It's an instinctive gesture born from a sudden need to anchor myself in this moment of unexpected happiness. To my surprise and relief, she doesn't pull away. Instead, her fingers intertwine with mine, giving a gentle squeeze that sends a warmth spreading through my chest.

A comfortable silence falls between us, and I find myself curious to learn more about Gabby. "So, tell me about your love for music," I say. "How did that start?"

Gabby's face lights up at the question. "Oh, it's always been a part of me," she says, her voice taking on a melodic quality. "I grew up in a musical family. For us, music was like food. We can't even go a few hours without it."

As she speaks, describing childhood memories of impromptu family concerts and lullabies sung in harmony, I'm struck by the passion in her voice. "That sounds wonderful," I say, a touch of wistfulness in my voice. "I can't even remember the last time I listened to the radio, let alone *made* music."

"Well, we'll have to see if we can change that." She nudges me.

Rose finishes her routine with a flourish, and the crowd erupts with applause. I have to admit, she's really good. She takes a playful bow.

"See?" she says, not the least bit out of breath as she returns to our table. "Sometimes you just need to dance it out."

"I want to dance like you." Leena bounces on her knees on the seat. "Can I, Daddy?"

Rose's face holds as much hope as Leena's. The woman must love to dance.

The idea of scheduling another activity into Leena's life and juggling my own schedule to accommodate it seems as probable as reindeer poop in my refrigerator.

"I don't think so. I don't have a way to get you to classes after school."

"I could take her," Gabby offers.

For a moment, I'm tempted to accept. But the rational part of my brain kicks in, reminding me of the dangers of becoming too dependent on others. "Thanks, but I can't ask for that kind of commitment from you," I say, perhaps more brusquely than I intend.

A flicker of hurt passes across Gabby's face before she turns her expression into a polite smile. "Of course, I understand," she says, rising from her seat. "If you'll excuse me, I need to freshen up."

As Gabby walks away, Rose turns to me, her blue eyes piercing. "You know, you can ask for help sometimes," she scolds me. "It doesn't make you weak."

I shake my head. Rose is nice enough, but she has a way of inserting her opinion into my life that grates on my nerves. "I'm better off on my own," I say, the words sounding hollow even to my own ears because recent events testify to the opposite.

"You are never alone," Rose says softly, and I feel the truth of her words warm my heart. It's been a long time since I've thought about my faith, about the constant presence of God in my life.

"Sometimes I forget to ask God for help, too," I admit, surprised by my own candor.

Rose smiles, a gentle, understanding expression. "God never forgets you," she says. Her gaze shifts to something over my shoulder, and I turn to see Gabby making her way back to our table. "You should let her into your heart," Rose adds softly. "She's a good person."

I don't trust myself to speak, and I'm afraid I'll say the wrong thing. As Gabby approaches, I feel a shift inside me, a softening of the walls I've built around my heart.

Just then, my phone alarm goes off. Leena's face falls. "Does this mean we have to go?"

I nod regretfully, already feeling the weight of responsibilities settling back onto my shoulders. But as I look at Gabby, I make a split-second decision.

"Are you ready to go?" I ask her, my voice warmer than before. "I'm sorry, but I have work to do tonight."

Surprise flickers across her face before she nods. "Yes, I'm ready."

As we walk to the car, I open the door for Gabby,

allowing Leena to climb into the back seat. Before I get in, I turn to Gabby. "Thank you for coming with us today," I say, meeting her eyes. "You made it more special."

She blushes. "Thank you. This has been... well, it's been wonderful." There's a moment of charged silence between us, filled with all the things we're not quite ready to say. I find myself leaning in slightly, drawn by some invisible force. Gabby's eyes widen, her lips parting softly...

"Daddy. It's cold," Leena admonishes me for keeping the door open.

I grin sheepishly, shut the door, and catch sight of my reflection in the glass. There's a lightness in my eyes that I haven't seen in years, a hint of the man I used to be before heartbreak and disappointment hardened me.

I take the long way through town, slowing down in front of the houses that have Christmas light displays out front so everyone can admire them. Gabby finds a Christmas music station on the radio, and we sing along to the songs we know and laugh at ourselves for not knowing the others.

Later, as I walk Gabby to her door, the night air crisp and cool against our faces, I find myself reluctant to say goodbye. We linger by her door, neither of us quite ready to end the evening.

"Thank you again for tonight," I say, my breath visible in the cold air. "It meant a lot to Leena... and to me."

Gabby smiles, her cheeks pink from the cold. "I

should be thanking you. I can't remember the last time I enjoyed pancakes this much."

There's a hint of something in her voice–loneliness, perhaps, or a longing for connection–that resonates deeply with me. Before I can talk myself out of it, I ask, "Would you like to come over for dinner tomorrow night? Nothing fancy, just... a chance to spend some more time together."

The smile that lights up Gabby's face is radiant, warming me despite the chill in the air. "I'd love that," she says softly.

"Great." I walk backward and smile at her. "I'll see you to–." My heel catches on a snowdrift, and I stumble backward. My arms windmill, and somehow, I manage to keep my feet–though I looked like a baby reindeer taking its first steps.

"Are you okay?" Gabby asks.

"I'm fine." I shake my shoe. "A little snow-packed, but good." The snow starts to melt, and my feet get wet. Great. "I'll see you later." I wave and head to the car, this time watching where I'm going.

"Did you have fun today?" I ask Leena as I get into the car.

Leena nods, her voice sleepy as she says, "It was the best day ever, Daddy."

That makes two of those in the last week. I'm on a roll.

The realization that Leena is so easily happy strikes me, and my throat closes off with emotion. For the first time in longer than I can remember, I'm looking forward to tomorrow. I can't help but think that all this time that I've been existing, God has wanted more for me, but I wasn't willing to reach for it.

I'm reaching now, I think, looking up at the inky dark sky full of silver clouds. *Please don't let me fall.*

Eight

TYLER

The soft glow of the television flickers across Leena's face as she snuggles deeper into my side on the couch, her eyes wide with wonder as Buddy the Elf navigates the streets of New York City. I glance up from my laptop, the harsh blue light a stark contrast to the warm, festive scenes playing out on the screen. It's well past eleven, and I know I should have put Leena to bed hours ago, but I can't bring myself to interrupt this rare moment of holiday fun.

"Daddy," Leena giggles, pointing at the screen. "He's eating cotton balls!"

I force a smile, trying to focus on the movie for a moment. "That's... interesting, sweetheart," I manage before my eyes inevitably drawback to the contract I'm reviewing.

This isn't how movie night is supposed to be. I know that. I should have popped popcorn and made some of that white-–chocolate cereal mix stuff my mom used to make every year. But by the time we got home from dropping off Gabby, I had seventeen emails and enough work to stay up all night. I'm doing my best even if it isn't enough. Somehow, the wave of guilt that would normally wash over me is not there. Maybe it's because we did the pancake dinner tonight already?

As the credits roll, I close my laptop with a soft click. "Time for bed. We've got church in the morning."

Leena yawns, stretching her arms above her head. "Will my new friend Rose be at church tomorrow?" she asks, her voice thick with sleep.

I pause, caught off guard by the question. Rose seems to pop in at the most unexpected times. I'm not even sure where she lives or her last name. It's funny that Leena thinks of her as a friend. "I expect she will," I reply, scooping Leena up in my arms. "She seems to turn up everywhere else, doesn't she?"

As I tuck Leena into bed, her eyelids already drooping, I can't help but wonder about Rose myself. There's something about her that I can't quite put my finger on—like she's a drifter or something without roots and a place to lay her head each night.

I shake my head at my ridiculous thoughts. Of course, Rose has a home. Probably in one of the new condos they built a few years back. Those were full of retirees looking to downsize and have fewer responsibilities so they could travel.

I need sleep. Unfortunately, I have a date with my laptop to finish up.

Sunday morning dawns bright and crisp, the kind of winter day that sparkles like glitter on snow. I find a parking spot in front of The Pampered Pooch on First Street. The windows are painted with images of dogs that grin and doggie treats that look like elves, stockings, and ornaments. For once, I'm glad someone isn't focused on Jesus and the nativity in their holiday sales. I'm sure it would feel strange to buyers to feed a wise man to their dog.

I chuckle at my offbeat humor. No way I'm sharing that joke with the owner. Sometimes, things are better left unsaid–even if they're kind of funny.

I spy the church steeple up the street and gulp. I need to rework my sacrilegious thoughts before we step into the church, so I'm not struck by lightning. With this many clouds in the sky, God has all sorts of ammo up there that he could send my way.

Leena takes my hand as we walk past Casa Ramirez, Hank's Department Store, the coming soon book store, and the diner before rounding the corner and going past the library before finally reaching the church. I like walking to church. It gives me time to refocus my thoughts.

Leena's hand is warm in mine as we climb the steps. Her red velvet dress looks festive and warm, and I'm double-glad that I ordered it online.

"Do you think Ms. Robinson will be here?" she asks,

her eyes scanning the crowd of people filtering into the church.

"I'm not sure," I reply, my own eyes involuntarily searching for a glimpse of chestnut curls. "We'll have to wait and see." My invitation to dinner tonight stands, though. I was half-hoped we'd meet up with her here and then move things back to my house, but I neglected to ask what her plans are for worship today.

As we step inside, the warmth of the church envelops us, along with the soft murmur of conversation and the faint strains of the organist practicing. The smell of wood polish and old hymnals fills my nostrils, bringing with it a flood of memories from my childhood Sundays.

And then I see her. Gabby is sitting alone in a middle pew, her face serene as she gazes up at the stained glass windows. The sunlight streaming through the colored glass casts a rainbow of hues across her face, making her look like a princess. She's wearing a Christmas dress made of navy blue, large pieces of jewelry, and boots that disappear under the hem of her dress. Her hair is down, and she has makeup on, including lipstick, which is difficult to take my eyes off.

Leena spots her, too. With a squeal of delight, she breaks free from my grasp and dashes down the aisle. "Ms. Robinson!" she calls out, throwing her arms around Gabby in an enthusiastic–and surprise–hug.

Gabby's face lights up with joy. I'm struck with the knowledge that she's truly happy to see my little girl. "Leena," she says, returning the hug with equal enthusiasm.

As I approach, Gabby looks up at me, her hazel eyes twinkling. "Good morning, Tyler," she says softly. Something in my chest tightens at the sound of my name on her lips.

"Good morning," I reply, suddenly feeling awkward and out of place. "Are you saving these seats?"

Gabby shakes her head, her smile widening. "Not at all. I'd love some company."

"Can we sit with you?" Leena asks, already clambering onto the pew.

"Of course," Gabby replies, sliding over to make room. Leena settles in between us, her legs swinging happily as she chatters about the movie we watched last night.

As the service begins, I find myself hyper-aware of Gabby's presence on the other side of Leena. The scent of her perfume, a light floral fragrance, wafts over occasionally–teasing me. I want to be closer to her.

We stand for the first hymn, and I'm struck by the sound of Gabby's voice, clear and melodious, rising above the congregation. Of course, I think to myself, she would have a beautiful singing voice growing up in a musical family. I like that I know that about her.

As we sit back down, I'm suddenly struck by how much space there is between us, with Leena in the middle. Without overthinking it, I scoop Leena up and settle her on my lap, scooting closer to Gabby until our hips touch.

I feel rather than see Gabby's surprise, but then she leans into me slightly, tucking her hand in the crook of my arm. The warmth of her body against mine sends a jolt through me, and I'm suddenly more aware of how close we are than I was a moment ago about how far apart we seemed.

As the pastor begins his sermon, I try to focus on his words, but my mind keeps wandering. I find myself imagining what it would be like to hold Gabby close. To wrap her in my arms and protect her from here until the ends of the earth.

I give myself a mental shake. This is the church, for heaven's sake. I shouldn't have these thoughts here, in all places. I force myself to face forward, fixing my eyes on the paintings and willing myself to listen to the sermon.

Even as I try to concentrate on the pastor's words about love and family during the holiday season, I can't help but be aware of Gabby on a whole new level. The way she nods along with the sermon, the gentle rise and fall of her breath, the warmth of her body next to mine— it all combines to create a sense of rightness, of belonging.

As the service comes to an end and we file out of the church, Leena tugs on Gabby's hand. "Are you coming for dinner?"

Gabby pretends to think about it. "I guess that depends on what you're having."

"Grilled cheese." Leena beams at me. "It's our Sunday tradition."

Gabby's eyes sparkle with amusement. "A Sunday lunch tradition? Is that a thing?"

I feel a blush creeping up my neck, but there's something in Gabby's teasing tone that makes me want to play along. "Well," I say, puffing out my chest in mock pride, "you haven't had my grilled cheese. It's the best thing I make."

Leena giggles. "It's the only thing he makes," she stage-whispers.

We all burst into laughter, and I'm struck by how natural this feels–like maybe this was the life I was meant to have all along.

"Well, in that case, how can I refuse? I'm looking forward to experiencing this famous grilled cheese."

As we drive home, Leena chattering excitedly in the back, I can't help but steal glances at Gabby in the passenger seat. The sunlight streaming through the window catches the auburn highlights in her hair, and her profile against the winter landscape outside is nothing short of breathtaking.

For the first time in longer than I can remember, I'm not thinking about the work waiting for me at home. Instead, my mind is filled with thoughts of melted cheese, easy laughter, and the warmth of Gabby's smile.

As we pull into the driveway, I realize with a start that I'm looking forward to this more than I've looked forward to anything in a long time. The thought should frighten me, this sudden shift in my carefully ordered world. But as I watch Gabby help Leena out of the car, their heads bent together in conspiratorial whispers, I find that I'm not scared at all.

Instead, I feel a sense of anticipation, of possibility. It's as if a door I thought was permanently closed has suddenly cracked open, letting in a sliver of light and warmth.

I'm pretty sure my grilled cheese is going to knock Gabby's socks off, and I really like the idea of her walking barefoot in my house.

Nine

ROSE

I take my seat in a pew already filled with angels. Some angels praise God for eternity; the rest of us gather on Sundays to do the same.

On any other Sunday, I would revel in this moment, my feet tapping out a joyful rhythm, my heart soaring with the angelic choirs that fill the vast space with their harmonies. Today, my feet are still, my hands clasped tightly in my lap as I struggle to focus on the words of praise.

My mind keeps drifting back to Earth, to Tyler and Leena, and to Gabby, who I believe could be the link between Tyler and Leena–the tie that binds them all together. Tyler has his moments as a dad, but Gabby has that unique female quality that softens edges and gathers hearts.

The words I spoke to Tyler before I left echo in my mind: "You are never alone." I can still feel the warmth that spread through him as the truth of those words sank in, the realization that God is always with him. I just don't know if the feeling was strong enough for him to act on. Will he open his heart to Gabby, to the possibility of love and the family that she represents?

I thought about attending services on Earth, but my heart wasn't in it. I need a *home*. I need the peace that comes from being near my Maker. I need to be on this side of the veil where darkness cannot penetrate.

The choir's voices swell, their tones resonating through the church and stirring something deep within me. I close my eyes, trying to lose myself in the music, to find the peace and certainty that usually comes so easily in this place. Even as the divine melody washes over me, I can't shake the knot of worry in my chest, and my feet stay still.

As the service comes to an end, I remain seated, lost in thought, as the other angels file out around me. The rustle of their robes and the soft patter of their feet on the shimmering floor creates a soothing background noise.

"I love worshiping. Don't you?" A cheerful voice breaks through my reverie, and I look up to see Melody, a cupid in training. Her black hair bounces as she slides into the pew next to me, her eyes sparkling with the joy that she wears like a battery pack. She's training to help people find the person who helps them reach their highest potential–their soulmate.

"I do," I agree, not wanting to say anything more for fear my anxiousness would leak out of me.

Melody's smile falters as she studies my face. "Rose?

What's wrong? You're so... still. I don't think I've ever seen you sit through an entire service without tapping your toes at least once."

I let out a shaky breath, grateful for her perceptiveness. "I'm just... worried," I admit, the words feeling inadequate to express the tumult of emotions swirling within me. Not to mention, we're angels. I trust my God, I do!––with all my heart. I just can't see how this situation will work out. I want to know each step before I take it.

Melody's eyes widen with understanding. "Oh! You're in the middle of your Guardian Test, aren't you? How is that going?"

I lift a shoulder in a half-hearted shrug, the movement feeling stiff and unnatural. "I don't know," I confess, the words tumbling out in a rush. "I left my assignment at somewhat of a critical time. I keep testifying to him, but I'm afraid I'm just coming off as annoying."

Melody's expression softens, and she gives my arm a gentle squeeze. "If you're speaking truth, then you can't go wrong," she says simply, rising from the pew. "Stay true, and it will all be well."

As Melody walks away, her words hanging in the air between us, I find myself grumbling under my breath. "Easy for you to say," I mutter. Let's see how she feels come February when she faces her final exam.

Even as the words leave my mouth, I know they're not fair. Melody's right, of course. If I can't trust in God's plan, how can I expect Tyler to do the same?

Taking a deep breath, I close my eyes and begin to pray, my words soft but fervent in the now–empty church.

"Heavenly Father," I begin, my voice trembling slightly, "I come to You with a heart full of worry and hope. I pray for Tyler, Leena, and Gabby–this little family that could be if only Tyler would open his heart. Please, Lord, give Tyler the strength to let down his walls, to see the love and joy that's right in front of him. Help him to understand that true strength lies not in independence, but in the bonds of family and love."

As I speak, I feel a warmth spreading through me, a sense of peace slowly replacing the anxiety that's been gnawing at me. Encouraged, I continue, "I pray that Tyler will come to value the precious gift of family, not just for Christmas, but for all the years to come. Help him to see Gabby's kindness and love for what it is–a blessing, a chance at the happiness he deserves. And Lord, please watch over Leena. Let her father's love for her be the key that unlocks his heart to the possibility of a fuller, richer life."

Tears prick at the corners of my eyes as I continue, my words flowing more freely now. "I know I can't interfere with Tyler's free will, Lord. But I pray that You will guide him, that You will open his eyes to the joy and love that surrounds him. Help him to choose the path that will bring him happiness, even if it's the one that scares him the most."

As I finish my prayer, I feel a weight lift from my shoulders. The worry isn't gone completely–I don't think it will be until I know for certain how things turn out for Tyler and his family—but it's no longer the overwhelming force it was before.

I open my eyes, taking in the beauty of the church with renewed appreciation. The walls seem to pulse with divine energy, and I swear I can hear the faintest echo of the choir, a reminder of the constant presence of God's love.

For the first time since the service ended, I feel a smile tugging at the corners of my mouth. "Thank You," I whisper, my heart filled with gratitude. "For listening, for understanding, and for the reminder that *I* am never alone in this journey."

As I finally rise from the pew, I feel a renewed sense of purpose. I may not be able to control what happens on Earth, but I can trust in God's plan and in the power of love to transform even the most guarded of hearts.

With a final glance around the church, I make my way towards the pearlescent doors.

As I step out onto the Avenue of Serenity, the celestial light of Heaven warm on my face, I find myself humming a tune. My feet begin to move of their own accord, tapping out a rhythm on the gleaming street.

Before I know it, I'm dancing, my steps echoing the prayer of gratitude in my heart. Each tap, each twirl, is a hope for Tyler and his family. As I dance, I feel a connection to the earthly realm below, as if my steps are sending ripples of love and encouragement down to those I've left behind.

Other angels pause to watch, some smiling, others

shaking their heads in fond exasperation at my impromptu performance. But I don't care. This is who I am, how I express the joy and love that fills my being.

As my dance comes to an end, I'm exhilarated. The worry that had been weighing me down has transformed into a bubbling excitement, a certainty that somehow, someway, things will work out as they should. Maybe not as I planned, but exactly how God wants them to be.

Ten

TYLER

Sunday afternoon traffic wasn't bad. I pull into the driveway. The drive home felt like an eternity, even though we finished in under ten minutes. The afternoon sun casts long shadows across the snow-covered lawn, highlighting the bare spots where holiday decorations should be. I can't help but feel a twinge of embarrassment as I notice the contrast between our unadorned home and the festive displays of our neighbors. What will Gabby think of me without even a wreath on my front door? I'm as good as Ol' Scrooge, who thought it was all a waste of time and money.

Except, that's not how I feel, even if it's how I look. Don't judge a book... right?

Gabby's car pulls up behind mine, and I suddenly become acutely aware of the state of our home on the inside. Yikes! Last night's impromptu movie party with Leena left the living room in disarray, and I silently chastised myself for not tidying up this morning. I wasn't expecting a guest.

Now, I have two reasons to cancel this impromptu get-together and absolutely no inclination to do so. If Gabby wants perfect, she'll be sorely disappointed. If she's looking for a grilled cheese experience like she's never had before, I'm positive we'll deliver.

Leena and I hop out of the car.

"Ready for the world-famous Olsen grilled cheese?" I ask, trying to mask my self-consciousness as we make our way to the front door.

Gabby's warm laugh eases some of my tension. "I can't wait," she says, her eyes twinkling. "I've been dreaming about it since church."

I unlock the door, and Leena darts past us, her excitement palpable. "Can I show Ms. Robinson my room?" she asks, already tugging on Gabby's hand.

"Let's get changed out of our church clothes first, sweetie," I say, grateful for the chance to delay Gabby's full view of our lived-in home. "Why don't you go upstairs and put on something comfy? We'll start on lunch."

Leena nods and races up the stairs, her footsteps echoing through the house. As her bedroom door slams shut, I suddenly realize that Gabby and I are alone for the first time... in my home... where I live... No one's been in here but the babysitter, Leena, and me since the divorce. Wow—that's really strange, isn't it? Shouldn't I have friends or something? The awareness of how out of it I've been sends a jolt of nervous energy through me.

"So," I say, gesturing towards the kitchen, "shall we get started on those sandwiches?"

Gabby follows me into the kitchen and I busy myself pulling out ingredients and the electric fry pan. I watch her out of the corner of my eye as she takes in our kitchen. The small dining table is cluttered with Leena's art projects and my work papers, and the countertops are far from spotless. There's cereal scattered where Leena poured her own bowl, and the garbage is overflowing.

If Gabby notices any of this, she doesn't let on.

Instead, her attention is drawn to the refrigerator, covered in Leena's artwork and school photos. "These are wonderful," she says, her fingers lightly tracing a crayon drawing of what I think is supposed to be stick figures of Leena and me, standing next to our house.

"Leena's quite the artist," I say, feeling a surge of pride. "She gets that from her mother."

The words are out before I can stop them, and I freeze, waiting for the usual pang of hurt that accompanies any mention of Sarah. But to my surprise, it doesn't come. Instead, I find myself smiling at the memory of Leena's first finger-painted adventures on her high chair tray.

Gabby turns to me, her expression soft. "She's a very special girl," she says. "You've done an amazing job with her, Tyler."

The sincerity in her voice catches me off guard, and I feel a warmth spreading through my chest. "Thank you," I manage, suddenly finding it hard to meet her gaze. "She makes it easy."

Clearing my throat, I move to gather the ingredients for our lunch. "Alright, let's see what we've got here. Bread, butter, cheese..."

Gabby seamlessly steps in to help, taking the butter and beginning to spread it on the bread slices I've laid out on a cutting board. Our hands brush as I reach for the cheese, and I feel that same jolt of electricity I experienced in church.

"What's your secret ingredient?" Gabby asks.

I can't help but grin. "Since you're part of the grilled cheese inner circle now, I suppose I can let you in on it." I lean in conspiratorially. "It's brown mustard."

Gabby's laugh fills the kitchen, bright and melodious. "Mustard? In a grilled cheese?"

"Don't knock it 'til you've tried it," I say, enjoying the way her eyes crinkle at the corners when she smiles. "It adds a little bite that takes it to the next level. Also, Texas toast bread is a must."

As we work side by side, assembling the sandwiches and heating up the griddle, I'm struck by how natural this feels. The kitchen, usually a place of rushed meals and microwaved leftovers, is filled with warmth and laughter. The sizzle of butter on the hot griddle mingles with the scent of melting cheese, creating a homey atmosphere I haven't experienced in years. I fall into it like a kid in the ball pit, letting it wash over the top of me until I'm so deep I'd have to swim to get out.

Leena bounds back into the kitchen, now dressed in her favorite princess pajamas. "Can I help?" she asks, climbing onto a chair to watch us work.

"Of course, sweetie," Gabby says, handing her a plastic knife. "Why don't you help me spread some more butter on the bread?"

I watch as Gabby guides Leena's hand, showing her how to evenly coat the bread without tearing it. The sight of them together stirs something deep within me. It's a picture of family, of the kind of life I once thought was lost to me forever.

I hadn't thought of finding someone else to build a life with because I was so busy trying to hang on by my fingernails. Gabby sort of snuck up on me. Now that she's here, I realize that I brought her into my life *and* Leena's circle. Maybe I should have treaded more lightly or considered the consequences, but I didn't. I acted on a gut feeling and my own desires. Before I can berate myself, Gabby puts her arm around Leena and praises her for a job well done. Leena grins. I guess if I was going to blindly fall into a situation, I was blessed to fall into Gabby.

I don't want to spend a lot of time comparing her to Sarah, but the differences are so glaring that it's hard not to notice. Sarah wanted to be a trophy wife. Her beauty appointments, training at the gym, and shopping added up to a part-time job. One she resented taking time away from to have a baby. Gabby, on the other hand, is a natural beauty. She wears makeup, and her hair is shiny and beautiful, but it all looks effortless. Maybe that's because she's happy from the inside out, not from the outside. It's so very attractive that I can't help but gravitate towards her.

Leena puts the baby carrots and strawberries on the table—our standard side dishes for Sunday lunch.

As we sit down to eat, I make sure we're in the two closest chairs. The table is small, and we continually brush up against one another. It's thrilling. Every accidental touch jolts through me and makes me smile.

The first bite of my grilled cheese sandwich transports me back to my childhood. The crispy, buttery exterior gives way to gooey, melted cheese and the hint of brown mustard, adding just the right amount of zing. But it's more than just the taste—it's the company, the laughter, the sense of belonging that makes this simple meal feel like a feast.

"Okay. I give—this is pretty good," Gabby says, her eyes closed in appreciation as she savors her sandwich.

Leena nods enthusiastically, a string of cheese dangling from her chin. "Daddy makes the best-grilled cheese ever!"

I feel a flush of pride at their praise, but it's more than that. For the first time in longer than I can remember, I feel truly present in the moment, not thinking about work or worrying about the future. I'm just here, enjoying a meal with my daughter and this wonderful woman who has somehow found her way into our lives.

After lunch, we move to the living room, where our bare Christmas tree mocks me. Gabby was there when we picked it out. "I bet your tree is covered in decorations." I rub the back of my neck, which is burning.

She smiles. "It's not too shabby." She pulls out her phone and shows me and Leena a picture. "These red ones," she enlarges the picture so we can see the ornaments, "were my grandmothers."

"We don't have other people's ornaments," Leena tells her. "All ours came from Walmart."

My neck burns all the hotter. "I've, uh, been meaning to decorate it," I start to explain, but Gabby cuts me off with a smile.

"What are we waiting for?" she says, her eyes sparkling with excitement. "I have some time, and I love decorating trees."

"Really?!" Leena squeals. "The decorations are in here."

As Leena leads Gabby to the closet where we store our meager collection of Christmas decorations, I'm struck by how easily she fits into our home. She doesn't judge or criticize–she just jumps in, ready to help or make our holidays better.

We spend the next hour decorating the tree, and I find myself relaxing more with each passing minute. I dread wrapping the lights, but Gabby stands on one side of the tree, and I stand on the other, and we pass the strand back and forth under the direct supervision of my daughter. We started at the top and are working our way to the plug near the bottom of the tree.

"Move up, Daddy, there's a hole," Leena tells me.

I adjust the strand. "If we put them too close, we'll run out." I look through the branches to see Gabby grinning back at me.

"Wouldn't that be a unique memory," she says.

I'm struck by her easy acceptance of the imperfect. A

unique memory. A treasure. A moment in time that will never be forgotten. Isn't that what I want? Isn't that what we all want? Beautiful imperfection.

The tree lights up, and Leena gasps. "It's beautiful."

I step back and take it in. We used every strand in the storage box, and I have to admit that the tree looks impressive.

"These ones now!" Leena grabs for the ornaments, lifts the box, and the bottom falls out, scattering plastic baubles across the hardwood floor. Her eyes widen in shock.

I laugh. She looks at me like I've grown a third arm. I scoop her and the box up and squeeze her until she giggles. "I'll find them. You two can hang them, okay?"

"Okay." She smiles at me, and I feel like I've won the day.

Gabby and Leena take turns hanging ornaments while I crawl around on the floor, pulling ornaments out from under the side table and the sofa.

At one point, Leena holds up a handmade ornament–a popsicle stick frame with a photo of her as a toddler. "Where should we put this one, Daddy?"

I take the ornament from her, and my throat is suddenly tight as I look at the picture. It was taken just before Sarah left, one of the last happy moments we had as a family. For a moment, I'm transported back to that day. I feel a gentle hand on my arm. I look up to see Gabby watching me, her eyes full of understanding. "Why don't we put it right in front, where everyone can see it?" she suggests softly.

I nod, grateful for her intuition and understanding. She doesn't know my story, not the whole thing, but her heart is big enough to offer me kindness. As I hang the ornament on a prominent branch, I reach over and take Gabby's hand. She squeezes it before letting go and accepting an ornament for a higher branch from Leena. Something shifts inside me. The memory is still there, but it doesn't hurt quite as much. Instead, I find myself focusing on Leena's bright smile in the photo, on the joy she brings to my life every day.

We step back to admire our handiwork. There are open boxes scattered across the furniture and floor–a pile of hooks on the mantle and packaging in odd places, but it feels like a home. The twinkling lights reflect off the ornaments, casting a warm glow around the room. The scent of pine fills the air, mingling with the lingering aroma of our grilled cheese lunch.

"It's beautiful," Gabby says, her voice soft with awe. "You've done a wonderful job."

"We've done a wonderful job," I correct her, surprising myself with the warmth in my voice. "We couldn't have done it without you."

Leena tugs on Gabby's hand. "Can we make hot chocolate? Please?"

I start to say that we should probably call it a day, but the hopeful look on Leena's face stops me. "You know what? That sounds perfect. What do you say?" I ask Gabby.

Gabby's smile is answer enough. We head back to the kitchen, where I pull out the ingredients for hot chocolate. As I heat the milk on the stove, Gabby and Leena set about making a batch of instant vanilla pudding for dessert. Leena stands on a chair, carefully stirring the pudding mixture under Gabby's watchful eye. I find myself mesmerized by the domesticity of the scene, by how right it feels to have Gabby here with us, and how much I like it. I feel like I've stepped out of my reality and into a new and better one. Or maybe this was the one I was aiming for, and I got pushed off for a bit.

We settle back in the living room with our hot chocolate and pudding, a random combination, but somehow it works. Leena regales us with stories from school, her animated gestures nearly upsetting her mug of cocoa more than once. Gabby listens attentively, asking questions and laughing at all the right moments.

As the afternoon wears on, I realized with a start that I haven't thought about work once since we got home from church. The briefs waiting for my review, the emails piling up in my inbox–none of it seems as pressing as it did this morning. That's new for me. It's also been huge in reducing my stress levels. The knot that usually sits in my stomach isn't there.

When Gabby finally says she should be going, Leena's face falls. She throws her arms around Gabby's waist, burying her face in her sweater dress. "Do you have to go?" she asks, her voice muffled. "It's better when you're here."

I start to admonish Leena for being clingy, but the words die on my lips as I see the look on Gabby's face. There's a softness there, a mixture of surprise and affection that makes my heart skip a beat. She loves my daughter. The knowledge is like a snow drift landing on my head. Gabby truly and sincerely loves Leena.

"She's right," I say softly. "It's better when you're here."

Gabby's eyes dart to mine, searching for sincerity. I pray she can find it because I feel the words all the way to my toes. Her shoulders soften and she hugs Leena a little tighter. I place a hand on her shoulder, wanting to be close but aware that we have a little girl between us.

"I had a wonderful afternoon," Gabby says, her tone implying that she wants to say more but is holding back. My mind races with the possibilities, and my heart lifts.

"Leena, honey, let Gabby go," I say gently, even as I find myself wishing she could stay longer, too. "We've taken up enough of her Sunday already."

Gabby kneels down to Leena's level, brushing a strand of hair from her face. "I will see you tomorrow at school. We have to practice, practice, practice." She taps Leena's nose, earning a giggle.

"Okay," Leena agrees.

I offer Gabby a hand to help her stand. She takes it, and a warm current surges up my arm and zaps my heart. I'm suddenly overcome with the urge to do something, to acknowledge the specialness of this day. Before I can overthink it, I lean in and press a soft kiss to her cheek. "Thank you," I murmur, "for everything."

Gabby's cheeks flush a delightful shade of pink, and for a moment, we just stand there, caught in each other's gaze. Then she smiles, a smile that seems to light up her entire face, and heads out the door.

As I close the door behind her, I lean against it, my heart racing. That was ... unexpected ... great ... not enough ...

"Daddy?" Leena's voice breaks through my reverie. "Do you like Ms. Robinson?"

I look down at my daughter, her blue eyes wide and curious. For a moment, I consider deflecting, giving her some vague answer. But the events of the day–the laughter, the warmth, the sense of rightness I felt with Gabby here–are still too fresh, too real to deny.

"Yes, sweetheart," I say softly. "I do like her."

Leena's face breaks into a wide grin. "I like her too," she says. "Can she come over again soon?" She asks as if it's as easy as arranging a playdate with one of her friends.

Maybe it is.

I ruffle her hair. My heart is both warmed and terrified by her enthusiasm. "We'll see," I say, not wanting to make promises I'm not sure I can keep.

As Leena skips off to play in her room, I'm left alone with my thoughts. I do like Gabby–more than I've liked anyone in a very long time.

Leena's already so attached to her. If things don't work out if Gabby leaves like Sarah did... I'm not sure I could bear to see Leena's heart broken again.

With a deep breath, I push off from the door and head to the kitchen to clean up. I glance at the clock and realize how much of the day slipped away. The warmth of the afternoon starts to fade, replaced by a familiar anxiety.

What am I doing?

Leena has grown attached to Gabby so quickly. The memory of her arms wrapped around Gabby's waist, begging her not to go, sends a chill through me. What if Gabby leaves? The thought of Leena experiencing that kind of heartbreak again is almost unbearable.

I lean against the counter, running a hand through my hair. We don't have any promises from Gabby. She's kind and seems to genuinely care about us, but so did Sarah once upon a time. And look how that turned out.

Even as these doubts swirl in my mind, another voice pipes up. Gabby isn't Sarah. The image of Gabby helping with the grilled cheese, laughing at my mustard "secret ingredient," flashes before my eyes. Sarah would never have done that. She was always more interested in her phone, in her own life, than in sharing those small moments with us.

Maybe Gabby is different. The way she jumped in to help decorate the tree, how she listened to Leena's stories with genuine interest, how she seemed to fit so seamlessly into our little family... it all points to someone who genuinely wants to be here.

But is it fair to ask her to stick around? I glance at my work bag stuffed with files I should be reviewing right now. My job demands so much of my time and energy. How can I expect Gabby to be happy with the leftovers of my attention?

Sarah certainly wasn't. "You're not meeting my emotional needs," she had said when she left.

Even if Gabby is different, even if she's willing to stick around, can I be the partner she deserves? Can I balance my career and family life in a way that would make her happy?

The thought of trying–and failing–to keep a new wife happy fills me with dread. The last thing I want is to hurt Gabby or disappoint Leena. Maybe it's better to keep things as they are to protect all of us from potential heartbreak.

I close my eyes, feeling torn between hope and fear, between the desire for connection and the instinct to protect myself and Leena from hurt.

All I know is that something has shifted, and I'm standing on the edge of a decision that could change everything. Whether I'm ready for that change–whether I'm capable of making it work–remains to be seen.

Eleven

ROSE

The sweet aroma of freshly baked doughnuts and brewing coffee wafts through the air as I arrive just outside Sweet Haven Bakery & Café. I draw in a deep breath, and it smells like a Monday. The early morning sun casts a golden glow on the frost-covered windows. I like the feeling of today. Mondays are a fresh start, a new chance mingled with a sense of determination to get to work. I Buffalo step–twice–to the door.

I've worn my favorite pair of tap shoes this morning. They have a triple-stacked heel and double-stacked hard leather outsole made in teal blue patent leather. Pure heaven!

The cozy interior of the bakery envelops me in its warmth, and my tap shoes click softly against the worn wooden floor as I make my way to a small table near the window, positioning myself for a clear view of the entrance.

Maggie Whitfield, the bakery's owner, catches my eye

from behind the counter and gives me a friendly wave. Her curly auburn hair is pulled back into a ponytail, and she is wearing a festive red and green scarf. I smile and wave back, marveling at the way she embodies the spirit of Christmas in her every movement. "I'll take one of everything."

She laughs. "Hungry this morning?"

"I'm expecting company," I tell her.

"I'll have that over in a jiff."

I settle into my seat, my fingers drumming a quiet rhythm on the tabletop as I wait for Tyler and Leena to arrive. They should be here any minute if my senses are right–and they always are.

After yesterday's day of rest and worship, I feel refreshed and refocused.

It helps that I checked in on things that happened while I was gone, and I know Gabby spent the afternoon with Tyler and Leena. All on Tyler's invitation. I mean, that's huge. He should be in such a good mood this morning. I'll sweeten him up with breakfast, and we'll have a nice little chat. I can see it now; today is the day we will finally click as a guardian angel and her charge. I can't help but ball change under the table.

The bell above the door chimes again, and I look up to see Tyler and Leena enter the bakery. Leena's golden curls bounce with each step, her blue eyes wide with excitement as she takes in the array of treats on display. Tyler follows behind, his expression a mix of fondness for his daughter and the ever-present weariness that seems to cling to him like a shadow.

I stand up, waving to catch their attention. "Good morning, Tyler. Leena! What a lovely surprise to see you here." It's a surprise for them, so I'm not lying.

Leena's face lights up with recognition. "Ms. Rose," she exclaims, rushing over to give me a hug. The pure, innocent joy radiating from her warms my heart, reminding me of the divine love that flows through all of creation.

Tyler's reaction is more reserved, a polite nod as he approaches. "Good morning, Rose," he says, his tone cautious. "Are you a doughnut fan?"

I smile brightly, gesturing for them to join me at the table. "Maggie's doughnuts are heavenly." I wink at my own little joke, though it's lost on Tyler. Maggie arrives with a tray of doughnuts and sets them on the table. "I ordered enough to share–care to join me?"

Leena's eyes widen as she looks over the mound of neatly arranged pastries.

Maggie pats Tyler on the back. "She can't eat all that on her own."

Tyler chuckles. "I suppose not."

As they settle into their seats, I can't help but notice the slight softening in Tyler's expression as he looks at Leena. Hmm. Something has changed. It's like the edge was taken off of him. Well! I'll just have to find out how that happened.

"So," I begin, keeping my tone light and casual, "how was your Sunday?"

"It was so much fun!" Lilu gushes, her words tumbling out in a rush. She selects a classic maple bar, takes a bite, and then talks with her mouth full. "Ms. Robinson came over, and we made grilled cheeses and played games. And guess what?" She leans in conspiratorially, her voice dropping to a stage whisper. "Daddy likes her."

I can't contain my excitement at this news, my toes clicking against the floor as I bounce. "Is that so?" I ask, beaming at Tyler, whose face has turned a delightful shade of pink.

"Leena," he says, his voice stern but not unkind, "remember what we said about sharing private information?"

Leena's face falls slightly. "Sorry, Daddy," she mumbles, but the sparkle doesn't leave her eyes.

I can sense Tyler's emotional walls rebuilding themselves brick by brick. He turns to me, his brown eyes narrowed. I suddenly feel as if I'm on the witness stand and about to be cross-examined. My toes stop tapping.

"Where are you from, exactly?" he asks, his voice low and controlled. "Do you have family in town? I always see you alone."

The challenge in his voice is clear, but I've come too far to back out now. I meet his gaze steadily. "I like to help people," I say softly. "I care about what happens to you and Leena."

"But why?" he presses, frustration evident in his voice. "We barely know you."

Leena tugs on Tyler's sleeve, her face creased with concern. "Daddy, don't be grumpy at Ms. Rose. She's nice."

I smile at Leena, touched by her defense. "It's okay, sweetheart," I assure her. "I understand why your daddy might be confused." I reach into my pocket and pull out a crisp bill, handing it to Leena. "Would you be a dear and go pay for our doughnuts?"

Leena's eyes light up at the responsibility, and she nods eagerly before scampering off to the counter. As soon as she's out of earshot, I turn back to Tyler, taking a deep breath. It's time for the truth–all of it. If I'm going to help him, I can't hide anything. He's too sharp to let details slide. Besides, this is a day of connecting. I can't do that, if I'm not honest–it's just not possible.

"Tyler," I say, my voice quiet but firm, "I'm an angel."

He stares at me, his expression a mixture of disbelief and exasperation. "A what now?"

"An angel," I repeat patiently. "Your guardian angel, to be precise. I've been trying to help you, but you're very stubborn about letting me in."

Tyler's eyes narrow, and I can practically see the gears turning in his head as he tries to process this information. His gaze drops to my feet, lingering on my tap shoes. "You're an angel?" he asks skeptically.

I nod, a small smile playing at the corners of my mouth. "Second class, but I'm working on moving up. You're kind of my final exam."

To my surprise, Tyler lets out a short, humorless laugh. "Of course," he mutters, shaking his head. "I get a newbie."

"Hey!" I protest, putting my hands on my hips in

mock indignation. "I'll have you know I have a solid C average."

Tyler raises an eyebrow. "That's supposed to impress me?"

I flap my hands, trying to explain. "It's different in heaven. C is for Celestial."

"What's failing?" he asks, his tone mocking. "An H?"

"Heavens, no," I reply, unable to suppress a small giggle at the thought. "Failing is nothing. You just don't get a grade. You don't move forward." I pause, meeting his eyes meaningfully. "Kind of like how you've been for the last three years."

Tyler's face darkens at my words, and he looks down at his half-eaten chocolate glaze with coconut flakes, grumbling something under his breath, "How would she know? Angel–ha!" I can sense the turmoil of emotions swirling within him–confusion, frustration, fear, and underneath it all, a deep, aching hope that I'm telling the truth.

"Tyler," I say gently, leaning in closer, "you weren't created just to survive. God wants you to be happy, to thrive, to grow, to feel joy."

He shakes his head, still not meeting my gaze. "I'm pulled in too many directions," he admits, his voice barely above a whisper. "If I want to get ahead at work, I need to spend more time there. But I need and want to be home with Leena, and after that, there's no time to pursue anything," he pauses. "Otherwise, What do I do?" He stares at me as if I have all the answers. I do. It would be so easy to tell him to quit his job, take something that makes less and demands less, and be happy at home. Now that I've revealed myself as an angel, any advice I give will carry more weight–life-changing weight. I have to be so careful that I don't break the number one rule.

My heart aches for him, for the impossible choice he feels he has to make. I understand the pressure, the desire to make sure Leena never suffers or wants for anything. I do! It's the same feeling I have for him. I want to draw all the pain and uncertainty out of his life so he can just be.

More than anything, I want to tell him exactly what to do, to guide him step by step towards the happiness and fulfillment he deserves. I can't do that because it has to be his choice. I press my lips together, choosing my words carefully.

"*You* have to choose your path." I sit up taller. "I can tell you that no one ever died wishing they'd spent more time in the office."

He snorts. "I've heard that old adage before. You know what they say in the office to that?"

I shake my head.

"They say that everyone who dies without making a partner dies with a pocketful of regret and a family full of debt."

I groan. "That's not true.

"It feels true," he grumbles.

"Tyler, it's not about *dying* right–it's about *living* right. And you're choosing to live as though everything depends on you." Did he hear nothing I said about not being alone?

Tyler's head snaps up, his eyes flashing with a mixture

of disappointment and anger. "It does." He stands abruptly, his chair scraping against the floor. "Well, Angel Rose–if you really are an angel–thanks for nothing."

As if on cue, Leena returns, carefully holding my change. She hands it to me with a proud smile, oblivious to the tension between her father and me.

"Thank you, sweetheart," I say, forcing a smile despite the heaviness in my heart. "You did a wonderful job."

Tyler gathers Leena's coat, his movements brusque. "Come on, Leena," he says, his voice tight. "We need to get you to school."

As they head towards the door, Leena looks over her shoulder, her bright smile in contrast to her father's stormy expression. She waves enthusiastically. I wave back, though I don't feel the enthusiasm I'm projecting.

The door closes behind them, and my shoulders sag. The mountain of doughnuts sits untouched on the table before me. It was supposed to be a happy surprise. I swipe my finger through some frosting. "Some surprise," I grumble. "Surprise, I'm an angel. Aaand . . . you're gone."

I've failed. Again.

Despite my best intentions, I've only succeeded in pushing Tyler further away. The weight of my mission presses down on me, heavier than ever. Leena deserves better than I've given them. Her sweet disposition should be nurtured, and her love for all people–and angels– should be protected.

As I sit there, staring out the window at the bustling

street beyond, I can't help but wonder if I'm cut out for this. Maybe I'm not meant to be a guardian angel. Maybe I'm destined to spend another century in training, watching from the sidelines as others earn their wings.

Where did my Monday morning optimism go?

"Maggie, these maple doughnuts are a miracle in my mouth," exclaims a happy customer.

I frown. A miracle?

Oh! Maybe . . .

I take the miracle card Henry gave me on the day I received my final assignment. I'd almost forgotten about it. I tap it on the table, unsure how to use it to Tyler's best benefit.

This one will take some thinking.

Twelve

TYLER

The soft glow of my desk lamp illuminates the mountain of paperwork before me, casting long shadows across my office. The hum of the copy machine filters in through the closed door. Dave, whose office is next door, booms a laugh, but he only uses it for clients. He's chatting someone up and working hard.

I should be doing the same. I just can't bring myself to pick up the phone and make any one of the dozens of calls I need to make.

Outside, snowflakes drift lazily past the window, a stark contrast to the tension I feel coiling inside me. I can't shake the conversation with Rose from this morning, her words echoing in my mind like a persistent melody.

"An angel, *pft*!" I mutter, tossing my pen down in frustration. It clatters across the polished surface of my desk, coming to rest atop a stack of briefs I should have reviewed hours ago. The ticking of the antique wall clock seems to grow louder, a constant reminder of the time slipping away from me.

I push back from my desk and begin to pace; my footsteps muffled by the plush carpet. The familiar scent of leather-bound law books and freshly brewed coffee does little to calm my racing thoughts. Rose's words about not progressing, about being stuck, hit closer to home than I'd like to admit.

She doesn't know what it's like to have a boss breathing down her neck.

I snort at the image that thought brought to mind. Of course, an angel's boss is ... Nevermind. There's no use thinking about her absurd claims. An angel in tap shoes? Yeah, right.

Still... what she said about living right, not dying right scratches like a one-size-too-small-wool sweater.

"There's only so much of me to go around," I say to the empty room, running a hand through my hair. My eyes dart between the intimidating pile of work on my desk and the clock on the wall. 5:30 PM. If I leave now, I could pick up Leena from her after–school program, maybe even surprise Gabby and invite them both to dinner.

The thought of spending the evening with them sends a warm flutter through my chest. I can almost hear Leena's laughter, see Gabby's soft smile across a dinner table. But as quickly as the image forms, reality crashes back in.

I glance at the stack of files, each one representing a client depending on me, a case that needs my attention.

I've already fallen as far behind as the firm will allow. Any farther, and I'm out the door. They don't care that I have a daughter. They don't care that I want to take a beautiful woman to dinner. They don't even care that it's Christmas. To them, I'm a machine that will be thrown out at the first sign of a malfunction.

I shake my head, trying to clear the depressing thoughts. This is ridiculous. I'm a grown man and a successful lawyer. I don't believe in angels or divine intervention. And yet... What if it's true? What if Rose really is an angel sent to help me?

Heaven knows I could use some divine intervention–pun intended.

Before I can talk myself out of it, I call out, "Rose?"

I hold my breath, feeling foolish.

This is so dumb.

I can't believe I'm doing this.

Do angels just show up when you call their names? She's not a genie. Although, I'd take one of those right about now. I look up. Maybe the ceiling will open up, and she'll fall into my office?

I picture Rose. It's more likely that she'd tap dance through the wall. I yank my gaze to the window. Flying?

This is ridiculous, and I'm wasting my time.

I lean over my desk, trying to find the spot where I left off.

Tap-tappity-tap-tap. "You called?" Rose leans over my desk.

I jump. "Gah!" I grab my heart. "How did you–?" I glance at the door. It's still shut.

I blink, not quite believing what I'm seeing.

She laughs. "You believe me, don't you?"

I adjust my tie. "I've always known there are angels. I just never expected to meet one in real life. Are there ... a lot of you?"

She laughs. "Oh, Tyler, you'd be surprised how many of us are around–especially this Christmas."

"Really?"

She nods. "I mean, we're always watching out for you. This," she circles her hand around, indicating the two of us, "is a special case."

I nod. "Riiiight. Because I'm your final assignment."

Her mouth opens and then closes. Then she nods. "Was there a reason you called for me?"

So many questions run through my head. How does this angel thing work normally? What does she mean they're always watching out for me? Do angels sleep? Eat? Does she wear tap shoes when walking on clouds? Wait, are the streets paved with gold?

I scramble to get to the point because if Rose really is an angel, and I'm starting to believe she is–then I don't know how long I have with her.

I hold out a hand as I ask, "You're an angel, right?"

She stands a little straighter, a hint of pride in her voice. "I am."

I gesture helplessly at the mountain of folders on my desk, the filing cabinet, and the chair. "Can you help me with this?"

Rose tilts her head, her expression curious. "Yes, but I hesitate?"

"Why?" I ask.

She takes a deep breath. "If you trust me. Because if I do this work, it will all be done perfectly in accordance with God's will."

I look at the overwhelming amount of work before me, then back at Rose. "That's the best recommendation I've ever heard. It would take a miracle to get it done!"

Rose's face lights up. "That's exactly what I was thinking." She reaches into her pocket and pulls out what looks like a shimmering, translucent card. "Are you sure?"

I think about the freedom that's on the other side of this mountain, of dinner with Gabby, of reading a bedtime story to my daughter tonight. "I'm sure."

"Let's make a miracle happen."

Before I can ask what she means, Rose waves the card, and suddenly, the office erupts into a flurry of activity. Papers flutter and fly about the room like a flock of startled birds. Pens dance across documents, signing and initialing of their own accord. Files zip through the air, arranging themselves neatly before flying out the door, presumably to their intended recipients, or they arrange themselves in my filing cabinets. The computer hums, the screen flashes different pages and documents, and emails are written and sent so fast I can't read the names on the screen.

I stand there, mouth agape, as months' worth of work is completed in a matter of minutes. The air hums with energy, and I swear I can smell a hint of ozone, like the air after a lightning strike.

As suddenly as it began, the whirlwind of activity ceases. The office is eerily quiet, save for the steady tick of the wall clock. My desk, once buried under a mountain of paperwork, is now clear and organized, with appointments added to the desk calendar in neat handwriting.

Rose brushes off her palms, looking satisfied. "All in a day's work," she says casually, as if she hasn't just defied the laws of physics, time, and lawyering.

I can't help but chuckle, relief washing over me like spring run-off. This is incredible. Better than any Christmas gift I've ever gotten. "What was that miracle card thing?"

"Oh," Rose says, her tone nonchalant. "We're allowed one miracle per assignment."

Weeks of late nights and missed dinners with Leena condensed into a few miraculous minutes. It is a miracle! "I can't tell you how grateful I am," I say, my voice thick with emotion. "Christmas suddenly seems–hopeful."

Before Rose can respond, the door to my office swings open. My boss walks in, his eyebrows rising as he takes in the scene before him. "Am I interrupting?" he asks, nodding towards Rose and smiling at her as if she's the most important client on the planet.

Rose steps forward, extending her hand. "I'm Rose, class two angel," she says brightly, shaking Brad's hand.

Brad looks at me, his expression a mix of confusion and concern. I can almost hear the unspoken question: Is she crazy?

Rose, seemingly oblivious to Brad's skepticism, grins

brightly. "I'll see you two gents later," she says, giving us a wink before tap dancing out the door.

I chuckle as I watch her go. At the end of the hall, she disappears. I shake my head in wonder. If I hadn't seen it with my own eyes, I might not have believed it.

Brad places a hand on my shoulder, and his expression shifts, becoming more serious. "I wanted to talk to you about the Wrangler case," he says. "I just reviewed your work. It's... well, it's some of the best I've ever seen. Thorough, innovative, airtight. I'm impressed, Tyler."

Instead of the fierce pride I would have expected to feel, I find myself thinking of Rose's miracle, of the time I've suddenly been given. What did she say? It would all be done according to God's perfect will. Well, it has to have been because Brad dishes out praise as often as Santa comes down my chimney.

"Thank you, sir," I say, echoing Rose's earlier words. "All in a day's work."

As Brad leaves, closing the door behind him, I sink into my chair, my mind reeling. The clock on the wall reads 6:15 PM. Leena's after-school program doesn't end until 6:30. There's still time.

I reach for my phone, my heart racing as I dial Gabby's number. As it rings, I glance out the window at the gently falling snow, the twinkling lights of the town square visible in the distance. For the first time in longer than I can remember, I'm happy. And that's a big deal for me.

"Hello?" Gabby's warm voice comes through the speaker, and I feel a smile tugging at my lips.

"Gabby? It's Tyler. I know it's late notice, but my evening just opened up and I was wondering... are you free for dinner tonight? With Leena and me?" We're a package deal, but I feel like Gabby is up for that.

"Sure," she chirps.

"I'll pick you up in a few minutes."

"What should I wear?"

"You're beautiful in anything," I blurt.

"Charmer," she teases, then adds in a warmer tone, "Don't be late."

"Wild reindeer couldn't keep me away." We hang up and I'm lighter just for having talked to her.

I gather my coat and briefcase. I pause, looking back at the now-clear desk. "Thank you, Rose," I whisper, feeling slightly foolish but genuinely grateful.

As I step out into the snowy evening, the cold air nips at my cheeks, but I barely notice. The world seems different somehow, as if Rose's miracle extended beyond just my paperwork.

I drive safely, not wanting to slide off the road and delay our plans.

I pull up to Leena's after-school program, and my heart lights with anticipation. As I walk into the building, the scent of children's art supplies and sugar cookies fills the air. I spot Leena immediately, her curls bouncing as she concentrates on a drawing.

"Daddy!" she exclaims when she sees me, her face lighting up with surprise and joy. She runs to me, throwing her arms around my legs. "You're early!"

I scoop her up, breathing in the sweet scent of her

hair. "I am," I say, my voice thick with emotion. "I thought we could go to dinner with Ms. Robinson. Would you like that?"

Leena's enthusiastic nod and bright smile are all the answer I need. As we head back to the car, Leena chattering excitedly about her day, I feel a sense of rightness settles over me. This is living right.

Thirteen

TYLER

As I pull up to Gabby's apartment building, my heart races with a mixture of excitement and nervousness. The snow-dusted streets glisten under the warm glow of streetlights, creating a magical ambiance that feels fitting for this unexpected evening. I take a deep breath, steeling myself before I step out of the car. I haven't dated in so long that I sincerely question my abilities. It's not like riding a bike–don't let anyone tell you that it is. This feels so different, and I feel so awkward in my own skin–I wasn't this awkward at fifteen.

"Wait here, sweetie," I tell Leena, who's practically bouncing in her seat with anticipation. "I'll go get Ms. Robinson." I'm tempted to bring her with me just to break the ice, but I'm no coward. I refuse to hide behind my daughter's excitement. I have to do this on my own.

I make my way to Gabby's door, the crunch of snow under my feet really loud. Before I can knock, the door swings open, revealing Gabby wrapped in a cozy sweater, her hair hanging loose around her shoulders, and a

"Tyler," she says, her voice warm with welcome.

I grin. So far, so good. "Gabby," I reply. I drink her in. Her sweater is touchably soft and a dark green that makes her hair look red in the light. Her skin glows, and she's wearing a pair of ankle boots with a heel. I think she refreshed her makeup because it looks like she just put it on–which is awesome. I don't know why I'm thrilled that she took the few minutes she had to get ready to go out tonight–maybe because it's a sign she's excited to go, too?

I realize I've been staring at her for longer than is polite. I clear my head and my throat. "Are you ready?"

She steps out and locks her door before taking my arm. I didn't offer it, but the move is so smooth I feel like I did, and my chest lifts.

We walk to the car, our breath visible. My brain is as clear as a field after a big snowfall–no imprints, no thoughts, no nothing. I'm completely blank. Just when I'm about to panic that I'll never be able to have another thought again, I open the door for Gabby.

"Ms. Robinson!" Leena exclaims as Gabby slides into the passenger seat. "Daddy said we're going to dinner!"

Bless my little girl–she always has something to say.

Gabby turns in her seat to Leena, her smile radiant. "That's right, sweetie. Isn't it exciting?"

I shut the door behind her. *Exciting*. Dinner with me and Leena? Well, isn't that something? I glance up at the sky, wondering if Rose had anything to do with that little miracle.

I settle behind the wheel. We have a few restaurants in town and I'm not keen on driving into the city. "Diner food or Mexican?" I ask.

"Diner," Leena responds.

I wasn't asking her, but I was not going to tell her that. "That's one vote for the diner. What do you think?"

Gabby taps her chin. "I do like churros..."

Leena sucks in as if she just realized that she'd turned down one of her favorite desserts.

Gabby drops her hands in her lap. "But the diner has potato chowder, and I can't turn that down once I've thought about it."

"Yeah!" Leena throws her arms in the air, and Gabby laughs.

"Diner it is." I smile, enjoying the way these two make picking a restaurant seem like the best moment of my day.

I steal glances at Gabby whenever I can, marveling at how naturally she fits into our little world. Leena has several questions about the music they're playing in orchestra and Gabby takes time to go through each explanation. I'm trying to hide my grin when she catches me.

"What?" she shoves my arm.

"You have a teacher's voice." I snicker. "It's cute."

She lifts her chin. "My teacher's voice is not cute; it's authoritative."

"Oh, it's certainly that." I park the car. "I'm pretty

sure I could play *O Holy Night* after your explanation. I just think it's cute that you *have* a teacher's voice."

"I guess I can live with that." She gives me a saucy grin.

The local diner, Rosie's, is a staple in Benton Falls. As we step inside, the warm aroma of comfort food envelops us, mingling with the soft strains of *Silver Bells* playing from the vintage jukebox in the corner. We pick our own booth and slide in with Leena sitting across from me and Gabby. She seems to like this arrangement, as she has our undivided attention.

"Welcome to Rosie's," a cheerful waitress greets us. "Can I start you folks off with some hot chocolate? It's our special holiday blend."

"Yes, please," Leena exclaims before I can answer. I chuckle, nodding my agreement. Gabby asks for one, too.

"I'll be back in a minute." She leaves, and Gabby and Leena immediately huddle over the kids' menu. I watch, a warmth spreading through me as Gabby patiently helps Leena sound out the words.

"What's this one, Leena?" Gabby asks, pointing to a word.

Leena scrunches her nose in concentration. "Spa... spag... spaghetti!"

"That's right!" Gabby beams, high-fiving Leena.

I can't help but smile at the two of them. I also note that when Gabby helps Leena like this, she isn't using her teacher's voice. It's something else–something more personal and inviting; it's more like a mother's voice. I never thought about that kind of thing being attractive, but it makes me want to keep Gabby around.

Our hot chocolates arrive, topped with whipped cream and a sprinkle of cinnamon. Leena dives right in, emerging with a whipped cream mustache that sends us all into fits of laughter.

"So, Tyler," Gabby says, her eyes twinkling over the rim of her mug, "what prompted this impromptu dinner? Not that I'm complaining, of course."

I pause, considering how to explain the strange events of the afternoon. "Let's just say I had a... revelation of sorts. About what's really important."

Gabby tilts her head, curiosity is evident in her expression. "Oh? And what did you discover?"

I look at Leena, happily coloring on her placemat, then back at Gabby. "That I want more of this. More moments that matter with people I care about." I'm including her in that. I hope she understands.

Gabby's eyes soften, and she reaches under the table to squeeze my hand. The touch sends a jolt through me, and for a moment, I forget to breathe.

"I'm glad you had that revelation," she says softly.

The waitress returns to take our order, breaking the moment. We order, and then we're right back to chatting and laughing. Leena regales us with stories from school. Her hands gesture wildly as she describes the Christmas play they're preparing.

"And I get to be an elf!" she exclaims. "Ms. Robinson, will you help me practice my lines?"

Gabby's face lights up. "Of course."

Our food arrives steaming and delicious. As we eat, the conversation flows easily, punctuated by Leena's giggles and Gabby's melodious laughter. I find myself sharing stories from my own childhood Christmases, memories I haven't revisited in years.

"My dad used to jingle bells outside of my window on Christmas Eve," I confess, grinning at the memory. "I'd pull the covers up to my chin, squeeze my eyes shut, and hope Santa thought I was sleeping so he'd leave presents."

Gabby laughs, her eyes crinkling at the corners. "That's adorable. What about you, Leena? What's your favorite Christmas tradition?"

Leena thinks for a moment, twirling spaghetti around her fork. "I like opening presents."

"Me too," Gabby agrees.

As we finish our meal, I notice Leena's eyes starting to droop. She leans against the wall.

"I think someone's ready for bed," Gabby says softly, reaching over to smooth Leena's hair.

I nod, signaling for the check. As I reach for my wallet, I catch a glimpse of auburn hair and sky–blue eyes at a nearby table. But when I look again, the figure is gone. *Was that Rose?* I wonder, shaking my head in disbelief. I know she can show up at a moment's notice. If it was her, I hope she saw this moment, and that she believes the miracle was worth it.

The drive back to Gabby's apartment is quiet, Leena

fast asleep in the back seat. Gabby hums softly along with the Christmas carols on the radio, and I find myself wishing the drive would never end.

As I pull up to her home, I turn to Gabby. "Thank you for joining us tonight. It really meant a lot."

Gabby smiles, her eyes soft in the glow of the streetlights. "Thank you for inviting me. This was... really nice, Tyler."

There's a moment of silence filled with unspoken words and possibilities. Then, before I can overthink it, I speak. "Would you like me to walk you to your door?" I'm not just asking if I can walk her up and she knows it. There's an implication, in my words, an invitation.

Gabby nods, and I quickly check on Leena before stepping out of the car. The night air is crisp, our breaths visible in little puffs. I take her hand. It's small in mine, and our palms are warm together.

The Christmas lights adorning Gabby's porch cast a warm, multicolored glow across the fresh blanket of snow. Soft flurries dance in the chilly air, dusting our coats and hair with delicate crystals.

Gabby and I stand close, our breath mingling in visible puffs. Her cheeks and the tip of her nose are rosy from the cold, making her look even more adorable. My heart pounds against my ribs, every nerve ending alight. The air between us is thick with anticipation and unspoken desires.

Slowly, I reach up and brush a snowflake from Gabby's rosy cheek with my thumb, marveling at her beauty and the way she trembles slightly beneath my touch. Her eyes flutter closed. I cup her cheek in my palm as I lean in slowly, savoring every heartbeat of anticipation.

In a burst of courage, I close the remaining distance and press my lips to hers in a tender, chaste kiss. Our cold lips warm quickly from the shared heat. I relish the silken warmth of her lips the sweet taste of her peppermint chapstick.

She sighs softly and leans into me, resting a hand against my chest. I wrap my free arm around her waist, drawing her closer until we're pressed together, as close as we can get. I deepen the kiss, pouring every ounce of tenderness and hope I have for us into the connection, my thumb lightly stroking her cold cheek.

Gabby's lips move beneath mine, returning the kiss with equal passion, her fingers curling into the fabric of my coat as if she's trying to hold me there. The moment stretches on, perfect and infinite, a stolen slice of eternity.

As we part, snowflakes catch in our eyelashes. Gabby slowly opens her eyes, her lips curved into a blissful smile. I'm sure my expression matches hers. Reluctantly, I step back. "I'll call you tomorrow?"

Gabby nods, fishing her keys from her coat pocket. "I'll look forward to it. Let me know when you get home safe." I assure her I will. With one last smile, Gabby unlocks her door and slips inside.

I watch the door close, already feeling the lovely ache of missing her. Even when I'm back in my car, my heart is light, and my lips tingle. Leena is still fast asleep, and as I drive us home, I can't stop smiling.

This evening has been a gift, I realize. A chance to see what truly matters, to feel the warmth of family and the spark of new love. Before I fall asleep, I think to myself, *if this is living right, I want more.*

Fourteen

TYLER

The warmth from Gabby's gas fireplace envelops us, a stark contrast to the chilly December air outside. I can't help but notice it's not just the temperature that's different in here–it's the feeling. Gabby's home exudes a sense of comfort that I've rarely experienced since Sarah left, and I find myself relaxing almost instantly.

"Welcome!" Gabby ushers us into her living room. She's wearing a sweater again. I think she likes them and I'd bet that she'd like another one for Christmas. I saw one in the window of Hank's Department Store this morning that would match her eyes. I almost drove into a snowbank while staring at it because I could already see her in it, and she was beautiful. She *is* beautiful.

"Dinner's almost ready. Make yourselves at home."

I can smell gingerbread cookies. This woman is incredible. Work was a breeze today. Since Rose's miraculous help caught me up, anything that comes across my desk is now manageable. I accomplished so much today and was still able to leave in time to pick up Leena from her after-school program. We're having dinner with Gabby, and I don't feel the pressure to hurry up and get back to my computer. I'm free.

It's my Christmas miracle.

Leena's eyes widen with delight as she takes in the festive decorations adorning every corner of the room. A beautifully decorated Christmas tree stands proudly in the corner, its twinkling lights casting a soft glow across the space. Handmade ornaments and garlands hang from every available surface. Gabby wasn't kidding when she says she likes to decorate.

"Daddy, look," Leena exclaims, pointing to a collection of nutcrackers on the mantelpiece. "They're so pretty,"

I smile, running my hand through her soft curls. "They are. Why don't we go see if Gabby needs any help in the kitchen?"

We make our way to the kitchen, where the scent of roasting turkey and herbs grows stronger. Gabby stands at the stove, her chestnut curls pulled back in a messy bun, wisps escaping to frame her face. She turns to greet us, her warm hazel eyes crinkling at the corners as she smiles.

"Perfect timing," she says, wiping her hands on a festive apron adorned with dancing reindeer. "Leena, would you like to help me set the table?"

Leena nods enthusiastically, always eager to help. Gabby shows her where the silverware drawer is, and Leena gets to work.

"Can I help with anything?" I ask, feeling a bit out of place.

Gabby looks up, her smile warm and inviting. "Actually, could you grab the salad from the fridge? I just need to carve the turkey, and we'll be ready to eat."

"A whole turkey?" I ask. When she said she wanted to make us a holiday dinner, I didn't expect this much.

Gabby laughs. "It's been a couple of years since I've hosted something other than a girls' night or teachers' luncheon. I guess I got excited and went overboard."

There's something in her tone that hints at how happy she is to have us here. Not just because she likes us, but because we're what she wants. She's wanted a family. I stand behind her and put my hand on her hip. She leans into me–just slightly, but enough that I feel her desire for me. It makes me want to scoop her into my arms and never let her go.

I get close to her ear, close enough that I can smell the faint trace of vanilla on her skin. "Thank you. This is the best dinner we've had in ages," I say low, as I kiss her cheek.

She melts into me as if I've pushed some button inside of her that turned her bones to rubber. "Hmmm. I should cook like this more often," she teases.

I'm about to wrap my arm around her when I hear a handful of forks hit the table–reminding me that we're not alone. I give her one more quick kiss on the neck and then back away, needing some space to clear my head.

As we move around the kitchen, working in tandem to get dinner on the table, I'm hit with a sense of rightness that I haven't felt in years. The clink of plates, the sizzle of gravy on the stove, Leena's excited chatter–it all blends into a symphony of home and family that makes my chest tighten with emotion.

We sit down to eat, the dining table a vision of holiday cheer with its red tablecloth and centerpiece of pine cones and holly. The food looks and smells incredible–roast turkey with all the trimmings, crisp salad, and homemade rolls that steam when we break them open.

"This is amazing, Gabby," I say, genuinely impressed. I'm on my second helping of turkey, and I think Leena's eaten a half-dozen rolls.

Gabby grins. "Thanks. Leena, how's the play practice coming?"

Leena swallows and then launches into her lines. She stumbles on the fourth one and then stops. "I almost have them memorized."

"You do. You'll be ready." Gabby winks at her. "What was Christmas like for you growing up? Any traditions?" she asks me.

I find myself speaking more than I have in months, sharing memories that I want Leena to know about her grandparents. Ones I haven't thought of in years.

The meal is delicious, but it's more than just the food. There's a warmth here, a sense of belonging that I've been missing for so long. I watch Gabby interact with Leena, the way she gently wipes a smudge of gravy from my daughter's chin, and how she listens intently to every word as if it's the most important thing she's ever heard. And I feel something shift inside me, a loosening of the tight control I've held over my emotions for so long.

After dinner, we move to the living room. Gabby puts on a classic Christmas cartoon, and Leena settles in on the couch, her eyes wide with wonder as she watches the colorful characters dance across the screen. I find myself relaxing in the moment, the stress of work and responsibilities fading into the background.

As the cartoon progresses, I notice Leena's eyelids growing heavy. Before long, she's fast asleep, sprawled across the couch in the boneless way only children can manage. I move to wake her, but Gabby places a gentle hand on my arm.

"Let her sleep," she whispers. "She looks so peaceful."

I nod, realizing I don't want to disturb this moment, either. Gabby disappears into the kitchen, returning a few minutes later with two steaming mugs of hot cocoa. The rich, chocolaty aroma fills the air, mingling with the scent of pine from the Christmas tree.

"Here," she says, handing me both mugs. "I'll just tuck Leena in so she doesn't roll off the couch."

I watch as Gabby gently adjusts Leena's position, pulling a soft throw blanket over her small form. She smooths Leena's curls back from her forehead with such tenderness that I realize how much Gabby brings into our lives. The care and affection in that simple gesture speak volumes.

Gabby joins me on the loveseat, sitting sideways with her legs over my lap. She takes her cocoa and sips delicately. I put my arm over the back of the chair and play with the loose strands of her hair. We sit in comfortable silence for a while, sipping our drinks and watching the flames dance in the gas fireplace. The only sounds are the quiet crackle of the fire and Leena's soft, even breathing.

"I like the feel of your house," I say finally, breaking the silence.

Gabby turns to me, her eyes soft in the firelight. "That's one of the nicest compliments you could have given me," she says, her voice warm with pleasure.

I set my mug down on the coffee table, then gently take hers and do the same. Turning back to her, I find myself drawn in by the play of firelight on her features. I reach out, tracing the curve of her cheek with my fingertips. Her skin is soft and warm beneath my touch, and I feel a spark of electricity between us.

Slowly, giving her time to pull away if she wants, I lean in and press my lips to hers. The kiss is tender, soft, and gentle, filled with all the emotions I'm not sure how to express in words. To my relief, her lips move against mine with equal care and affection.

When we part, I rest my forehead against hers. "I'm falling for you, Gabby," I whisper, the words slipping out before I can second-guess them. I would have. I should have. I feel like I'm naked in a snowstorm–totally vulnerable and exposed to whatever she wants to throw at me.

"Me too," she replies, her voice equally soft. Then, with a small laugh, she clarifies, "I mean, I like you, Tyler. You're a good man."

Her words warm me from the inside out, chasing away the doubts and insecurities that have plagued me for so long. "I want to be," I admit. "I always feel like I'm falling short. Except with you. With you, I feel like I'm enough."

Gabby pulls back slightly, her eyes shining with emotion. "I take it back," she says, her voice thick. "*That* was the nicest thing you could have said to me."

I cup her face in my hands, marveling at how right this feels. "Can I tell you that you're beautiful, too?"

A slow smile spreads across her face. "I won't try to stop you."

We kiss again, and this time, it's deeper, filled with the growing feelings between us.

As we part, I glance over at Leena, still sleeping peacefully on the couch. The sight of her there, so trusting and vulnerable, in this warm and loving environment, fills me with a sense of belonging.

I turn back to Gabby, taking in her soft smile and the warmth in her eyes. For the first time in longer than I can remember, I feel hope blossoming in my chest. Hope for a future filled with more moments like this, more evenings spent with my girls.

The rest of the evening passes in a comfortable haze of soft conversation and shared laughter. We talk about everything and nothing–our childhoods, our dreams, our favorite holiday traditions. Gabby tells me about her passion for music, her eyes lighting up as she describes the joy of teaching children to play their first notes. I find myself telling her how I got into law to please my dad and then fell in love with it.

As the clock ticks towards midnight, I realize with a

start how late it's gotten. "We should probably head home," I say reluctantly, not wanting to break the spell of the evening. I wish I could stay. I wish I could hold this woman all night long and wake up to her in the morning. I don't want to leave.

Gabby nods, though I can see the same reluctance in her eyes. "Of course. Let me help you get Leena to the car."

We work together to bundle up my still-sleeping daughter, Gabby, who is holding the doors open as I carry Leena out to the car. The night air is crisp and cold, our breaths visible in little puffs of steam. Christmas lights twinkle on neighboring houses, and a light dusting of snow has begun to fall, adding to the magical atmosphere of the evening.

Once Leena is securely buckled in, I turn back to Gabby, who stands on her porch, arms wrapped around herself against the chill. I walk back up the path to her, drawn like a magnet.

"Thank you for tonight," I say softly, taking her hands in mine. "For dinner, for everything. It was..."

"Perfect?" Gabby supplies, a small smile playing at her lips.

I nod, squeezing her hands gently. "Yeah. Perfect."

We share one more kiss, soft and sweet, before I reluctantly pull away. "Goodnight, Gabby," I whisper.

"Goodnight, Tyler," she replies, her voice equally soft. "Drive safe."

I wait until she's safely inside before getting into the car. As I drive home through the quiet, snow-dusted streets, I can't stop smiling. The evening replays in my mind–the warmth of Gabby's home, the delicious meal, the tender moments we shared. But most of all, I think about the way Gabby interacted with Leena, the natural love that's grown between them.

For the first time in years, I allow myself to imagine a future–not just for myself but for all three of us. A future filled with family dinners, movie nights, shared laughter, and love. It's a quiet life. We'll travel, of course, but the majority of it will be in our home, together, sharing, laughing, loving, carrying each other's burdens, and eating really good food. It's a future worth fighting for.

I find myself looking forward to tomorrow–not for the work I'll accomplish, but for the possibility of seeing Gabby again, of creating more moments like the ones we shared tonight. I realize that I want to be the kind of man who is home for dinner every night.

Because tonight, in Gabby's warm and welcoming home, with my daughter sleeping peacefully nearby and the promise of new love blossoming in my heart, I felt peace. And I'm not about to let that go.

Fifteen

TYLER

Festive music fills the air, mingling with the excited chatter of families and the occasional blast of a trumpet from the approaching parade. Leena skips between Gabby and me, her mittened hand clasped tightly in mine, her eyes wide with wonder at the twinkling lights and colorful decorations adorning every storefront.

I don't know why the town picked the 22nd to host the Christmas Parade every year, but it's as regular as the clock tower in the town square. I've only come once before when Leena was a baby.

"I hear they have a new set of organizers this year," Gabby tells us as we weave through the crowd to find a place to watch. "They wanted to highlight local artists, so it should be interesting."

"Sounds like it." I grin over my shoulder at her as I squeeze through a small gap, Leena trailing behind and

Gabby taking up the rear. We get through, and our view of the street opens up.

"Look, Daddy," Leena exclaims, pointing to a group of carolers on the corner. Their harmonious voices rise above the general hubbub, singing a heartfelt rendition of "Silent Night." The sound stirs something deep within me. I feel like my emotion bottle has burst open, and I don't have a clue what comes up or when. I'm more sensitive to tender things. It's been great because I can feel a whole new level of love for Leena and all the wonderful things that Gabby stirs inside of me. It's also a bit concerning when I'm touched by a kind word from a client, and I have to swallow the ball of emotion in my throat.

I glance at Gabby, her chestnut curls peeking out from beneath a festive red hat, her cheeks flushed with the cold and excitement. She catches my eye and smiles, a warm, genuine smile that makes my heart skip a beat. It's hard to believe that just a few weeks ago, I was buried in work, barely noticing the holiday season passing me by. Now, here I am, in the heart of our town's Christmas Parade, surrounded by the spirit of the season and the two people who have come to mean everything to me.

"Here looks like a good spot," Gabby suggests, gesturing to a relatively clear area near the edge of the sidewalk. We position ourselves, Leena standing in front of us for the best view. Without thinking, I wrap my arm around Gabby's waist, drawing her close. She leans into me, and I'm struck by how natural, how right this feels. I hope I never get used to this feeling. At the same time I want to grow old with it.

The parade begins, a dazzling spectacle of lights, music, and holiday cheer. Floats adorned with twinkling lights and festive scenes glide by, each one eliciting gasps of delight from Leena and the other children lining the street. Marching bands play cheerful Christmas tunes, their instruments gleaming in the glow of the streetlights. Local dance troupes twirl by in glittering costumes, and community groups wave from decorated cars and trucks.

As we watch, I'm overwhelmed by a sense of community I haven't felt in years. I recognize faces in the crowd and on the floats–the baker who provides Leena's favorite cookies, my dental hygienist dressed as an elf, Gabby's fellow teachers from the high school marching with the school band. This is my town; these are my people, and for the first time in a long time, I feel truly connected to it all.

"It's the community orchestra!" Gabby exclaims, pointing to an approaching float.

Sure enough, a group of musicians glides by, playing a beautiful arrangement of *Carol of the Bells*. I spot several of Gabby's friends among them, and they wave enthusiastically when they see her without missing a note. Gabby waves back, her face alight with joy.

"Ms. Robinson!" Leena tugs on Gabby's coat. "Why aren't you playing with them?"

Gabby kneels down to Leena's level, her eyes twinkling. "Well, sweetie, this year, I wanted to watch the parade with you and your dad."

Leena throws her arms around Gabby in a spontaneous hug. Over Leena's head, Gabby's eyes meet mine, and I see in them the same wonder and gratitude I feel. How did we get so lucky?

As the parade continues, I find myself paying less attention to the spectacle before us and more to the two people beside me. Leena's enthusiasm, her gasps of delight at each new float or performer, fill me with a joy I'd almost forgotten I could feel. And Gabby... Gabby's presence feels like coming home after a long, tiring journey.

"Tyler? Gabby?" A voice breaks through my reverie. I turn to see Mrs. Thompson, Leena's kindergarten teacher, smiling at us. "What a lovely surprise! Are you three here together?"

For a moment, I'm taken aback by the question. In the past, I might have stammered, might have clarified that Gabby is just Leena's music teacher, a friend. But now, without hesitation, I find myself nodding.

"Yes," I say, tightening my arm around Gabby's waist. "Yes, we are."

I feel Gabby's slight intake of breath, and for a split second, I worry I've overstepped. But then she relaxes against me, her hand coming to rest over mine.

Mrs. Thompson beams at us. "How wonderful! Merry Christmas!"

As she moves on, I look down at Leena, worried about her reaction. But my daughter is grinning up at us, her eyes shining with happiness. "Can we get hot chocolate after the parade?" she asks, as if nothing out of the ordinary has happened.

"I'm game," Gabby replies.

In a lull between floats, my eyes are drawn to a familiar figure across the street. Rose. It's Rose! She's wearing those blue tap shoes; I can see the lights bounce off them from here. When our gazes meet, she smiles—a smile full of knowing and joy.

I raise my hand in a wave, mouthing "Thank you" to her. She nods, her smile widening, and gives me a thumbs up. Then, as another float passes between us, and when it's passed, she's gone.

As the last float goes by—Santa on his sleigh, of course—and the crowd begins to disperse, I pull Gabby and Leena close. "What do you say we go get that hot chocolate?" I suggest.

"Yes!" Leena cheers, bouncing on her toes.

Gabby looks up at me, her eyes soft in the glow of the Christmas lights. "That sounds wonderful," she says quietly.

As we make our way through the festive streets towards our favorite café, Leena skipping ahead and Gabby's hand warm in mine, I squeeze Gabby's hand gently, and she looks up at me with a questioning smile. "Thank you," I say softly.

"For what?" she asks.

I gesture around us—at Leena, at the festive town, at the warmth between us. "For this. For everything. For helping me remember what's really important."

Gabby's eyes shimmer with unshed tears, but her

smile is radiant. "Thank you for letting me be a part of it," she whispers back.

As we step into the warm, cinnamon-scented interior of the café, Leena is already chattering excitedly about marshmallows and whipped cream. I never want Christmas to end. I don't want to see what's on the other side of this season. I just want to stay right here, right now.

It feels like too much to ask for, but I'm going to pray for it, anyway.

Sixteen

ROSE

The celestial light of Heaven bathes my skin as I appear in the corridors leading to Henry's office. My tap shoes click-clack against the floor, creating a joyful rhythm that echoes through the hallway.

As I approach Henry's office, I can barely contain my excitement. I've done it. I've completed my assignment. Tyler, Gabby, and Leena are well on their way to becoming the family they are meant to be. I can almost feel my wings sprouting already.

Without bothering to knock, I burst through the door, my face split in a wide grin. "Henry!" I exclaim, my voice ringing with triumph. *Tappity-tap-tap* go my feet. "My assignment is complete!"

Henry looks up from his desk, his silver hair catching the light streaming through the window behind him. His blue eyes twinkle with amusement, but I detect a hint of skepticism in his raised eyebrow.

"Is that so?" he asks, his voice calm and measured. "And what makes you so certain?"

I tap dance in place, unable to contain my excitement. "You should see them, Henry. Tyler's finally opening up, letting love into his life. He and Gabby are perfect together, and Leena is thriving with all the love and attention. They're a real family now."

Henry leans back in his chair, his fingers steepled under his chin. "Well, that certainly sounds promising. Perhaps I should take a look for myself, hmm?"

He stands up and comes to stand beside me. "To Tyler's home?" he asks.

I nod. "Let's go." We close our eyes and then open them and we're standing in Tyler's living room. The scene before us is one of domestic bliss–Tyler, Gabby, and Leena are curled up on the couch, laughing as they watch a Christmas movie together. The room is bathed in the warm glow of twinkling lights and the scent of freshly baked cookies.

My heart swells with pride as I watch them. "See?" I say, turning to Henry. "They're happy. They're together. Mission accomplished!"

Henry nods slowly, a small smile playing at the corners of his mouth. "It does look good," he admits. "Tyler seems to have come a long way from the work-a-holic, broken-hearted man he was."

I beam. "So, when do I get my wings? I'm ready to be a full-fledged guardian angel." *Tap-tap-shuffle-change-tap.*

Henry chuckles. "Not so fast, Rose. The archangel

won't be here until Christmas Day to hear your dissertation. You'll have to cool your tap shoes until he arrives."

My face falls, disappointment washing over me. "But... but I've done everything I was supposed to do," I protest weakly. "And that's three whole days away."

Henry's eyes soften with understanding. "I know you have, Rose. All things in God's time, yes?"

I nod, trying to hide my disappointment. "I understand," I say, even though a part of me doesn't really.

"Let's head back." We close our eyes and open them back in his office.

Henry places a comforting hand on my shoulder. "Perhaps," he suggests gently, "you could use this time to help a few more newly arrived angels? It could be good practice for your future role as a guardian angel."

The idea perks me up a bit. "That's true," I admit. "I do enjoy helping the newcomers adjust."

Henry smiles. "That's the spirit. Now, why don't you head down to your office? I'm sure there's someone there who could use your guidance."

With a nod and a grateful smile, I leave Henry's office, my tap shoes creating a slightly less enthusiastic rhythm as I make my way to the guidance counselor's building. The hallways are filled with the soft murmur of angelic voices.

As I enter my office, I'm greeted by the soothing blue walls and the comforting scent of blooming flowers. The cloud-like rug beneath my feet muffles the sound of my tap shoes, creating a serene atmosphere. I've barely settled behind my desk when there's a soft knock at the door.

"Come in," I call out, straightening up and putting on my best counselor smile.

The door opens and in walks Dr. James Richardson, the former pediatric surgeon I had assigned to be a celestial janitor in the Heavenly Mess Hall. My smile falters slightly as I take in his dejected expression.

"Dr. Richardson," I greet him warmly. "How can I help you today?"

He slumps into one of the cushioned chairs across from my desk, his shoulders sagging. "I'm miserable in my job, Rose," he confesses, his voice heavy with disappointment. "I thought Heaven would be ... better than this."

My heart sinks at his words, and my mouth falls open. I had been so sure that giving him a completely different role would help him embrace his new existence. "I'm sorry to hear that, James," I say softly. "Can you tell me more about what's troubling you?"

He sighs, running a hand through his salt-and-pepper hair. "I thought... I thought I'd be happier when I made it to Heaven. I thought everything would be perfect. But this job... it's just not fulfilling. I miss the challenge of medicine, the satisfaction of helping people."

I lean forward, my brow furrowed in concern. "But James, haven't you been trying new things? Exploring different aspects of yourself that you couldn't on Earth?"

He shakes his head dejectedly. "I've tried, Rose. I really have. But mopping floors and cleaning tables... it's just not me. I feel like I'm fading away."

I bite my lip, feeling a twinge of guilt. Had I been too hasty in my assignment? Too confident in my ability to know what was best for him? "James," I say gently, "sometimes it takes time to adjust to new situations. Even in Heaven, change can be difficult. Have you given yourself a chance to really embrace this new role?"

He looks up at me, his eyes filled with a mixture of frustration and disappointment. "I've been trying, Rose. But every day feels the same."

His words hit me like a thunderbolt. It's what Tyler felt like before I lightened his load with the miracle. "I... I see," I manage to say, trying to keep my voice steady. "What would you like to do?"

James leans back in his chair. "I think I'd like to do what you're doing."

I blink so fast I can see my own eyelashes. "You want to be a *guidance counselor*?" I only took the position because I thought it would be good training to become a guardian angel.

He nods. "I think I'd be good at it."

Now, it's my turn to lean back in my chair. "I don't see why you couldn't try." I find the right paperwork in my desk drawer. Yes, there's still paperwork in heaven. We are a place of order. I didn't want to share that information with Tyler, as I think it would have disheartened him. Some angles and people love filing things in their proper place. I'm one of those angels. "Take this down the corridor to the receptionist, and she'll enroll you in the introductory courses. It shouldn't take long for you to start."

James stands, his shoulders back and his face eager. "Thank you. I promise I won't let you down."

"I believe you. Congratulations on your new calling." I say all the right things, but my mind is in turmoil. How could I have been so wrong about James? I was so sure that giving him a completely different role would help him find joy and purpose in Heaven. But instead, he was miserable.

I was also certain about using the miracle to help Tyler. The image of Tyler, Gabby, and Leena curled up together comes back to me, and I relax. The miracle was done in accordance with God's Laws and Will. I can't mess that up.

With renewed determination, I turn back to my desk, ready to face whatever challenges come my way. After all, isn't that what being a guardian angel is really about? Not just solving problems, but walking alongside souls as they navigate their own journeys. The situation with James was a fluke. Nothing to worry about.

As I settle in to review my notes on the newly arrived souls, I can't help but smile.

I just have to bide my time until the archangel arrives, and then I will get my wings.

Everything will be fine.

Seventeen

TYLER

The soft glow of the morning sun filters through the frost-covered windows of my office, casting a warm light across the polished surface of my desk. It's early enough that the smell of coffee is warm and fresh and not stale and sad.

December 23rd and the office is already humming–people want to get their work done and get home, so they'd rather come in before the sun is up. I don't blame them. I came as soon as my babysitter could get to my house. She wasn't happy about not being able to sleep in over Christmas break, but I promised I'd pay her double today, so she dragged herself over.

I lean back in my leather chair, a contentment settling over me that I haven't felt in years. Tomorrow is Christmas Eve, and for the first time since Sarah left, I'm actually looking forward to the holiday. The thought of spending it with Gabby and Leena fills me with a warmth that has nothing to do with the coffee in my hand.

A smile tugs at my lips as I recall Gabby's offer to help wrap gifts on Christmas Eve after Leena goes to bed. The prospect of spending time alone with her, even if it's just to tackle the mountain of presents I've bought for Leena, sends a thrill through me.

I glance at the framed photo of Leena on my desk, her gap-toothed grin beaming up at me. The love I feel for my daughter has always been a constant, but now it feels like it's expanding, growing to include Gabby in a way I never expected. If things continue along this path, then Gabby will be a permanent part of our lives before Valentine's Day. I'm not someone who likes to stay in limbo—even though I've lived there since Sarah left. Once I make up my mind, I want to take action. I don't think Gabby will want a long engagement, either. Her family is far away, and they all have their own lives. Her parents are retired and can work around our schedule, as are mine. A small ceremony will be enough and everything all at once.

"Tyler!" my boss yells from his office down the hall. I blink out of my daydreams in just enough time to stand as he storms through my door.

Without a word, he tosses a file onto my desk with enough force to send my pencil holder rattling. "What is this?" he demands, his voice tight with barely controlled fury.

Confused, I lower my eyebrows. "I'm not sure," I admit, flipping it open. My heart sinks as I recognize the contents. It's one of the files Rose used her 'miracle card' on, the one she assured me was handled according to "God's will." But as my eyes scan the document, I realize with growing horror that something has gone terribly wrong.

The purchase price listed is significantly lower than what our client had agreed to. My stomach churns as I realize the implications. "Uh, that's not right," I stammer, looking up at Brad. Our client was very specific about the asking price for their business, refusing to budge. They've already turned down several offers that were more than fair considering the last two years' of profits–or, I should say, lack of profits.

His eyes are hard as flint as he glares down at me. "It's not," he agrees, his voice cold. We stood to make a tidy sum in this if it was handled properly. "And now it's signed. You'd better fix this." Without another word, he turns on his heel and storms out, leaving me alone with the evidence of my carelessness.

I groan, dropping my head into my hands. This is a disaster. Fixing this will mean hours of phone calls, emergency meetings, and possibly even legal action if we can't sort it out amicably. The thought of all the work ahead–and everything I'll miss this Christmas–makes my head throb.

With a heavy heart, I reach for my phone. My fingers hover over Gabby's number for a moment before I force myself to dial. The sound of her warm voice answering fills me with both comfort and guilt.

"Tyler! I was just thinking about you. Are you calling to add anything to our menu list for tonight?"

I close my eyes, hating myself for what I'm about to say. "Actually, Gabby, that's why I'm calling. There's been a problem at work. A big one. I... I'm going to be late tonight."

There's a pause on the other end of the line, and I can almost see the disappointment on her face. When she speaks again, though, her voice is full of understanding. "Oh, I see. Well, don't worry about us. I'll pick up Leena and go to your place. We'll get started without you."

Relief washes over me, tinged with a pang of regret for missing out on time with them. "Thank you," I say softly. "I'm sorry about this."

"Hey," Gabby says, her voice warm and encouraging. "Hurry if you can, because it's not a party unless you're here."

Her words bring a smile to my face despite the stress weighing on me. "I'll do my best," I promise. "Save some cocoa for me."

As I hang up, the reality of the situation crashes back over me. I take a deep breath, steeling myself for the long day ahead. "Janet," I call out to my secretary. "I need you to get a client on the phone. It's urgent."

Janet's efficient "Right away, Mr. Olsen" floats back to me as I turn my attention to the file in front of me. The warmth and joy I felt just moments ago seems to evaporate, replaced by a familiar tension in my shoulders and a knot in my stomach.

As I dive into the messy details of the contract, a part of me can't help but wonder if this is some kind of cosmic joke. Just when I thought I had finally found the right balance between work and family, just when I was starting to believe that maybe I could have it all, I get a curveball.

As the hours tick by, I find myself drowning in a sea of paperwork and phone calls. The client is furious and is threatening legal action if we don't fix this immediately. My boss's disappointed face keeps appearing in my doorway as he hovers over me. Along with all that comes the realization that this mistake could cost me the partnership I've been working towards for years.

The sky outside my window has long since darkened to an inky black. I glance at the clock–9:30 PM. My heart sinks as I realize I've completely missed the evening with Gabby and Leena. The image of them waiting for me, their hopeful faces slowly giving way to disappointment, makes my chest ache.

I reach for my phone, dreading the call I need to make. Gabby answers on the second ring, her voice tinged with concern. "Tyler? Are you okay?"

I close my eyes, guilt washing over me. It's the same thing that happened before. I try to please everyone and no one is ever happy. "Gabby, I'm so sorry. There's been a major issue with a contract, and I... I'm not going to make it home tonight."

The silence on the other end of the line is deafening. When Gabby finally speaks, her voice is soft and understanding, but I can hear the disappointment she's trying to hide. "Well, don't worry about us. I'll sleep on your couch so Leena can be in her bed, and we'll make a girls' night of it."

I breathe out. Knowing Gabby is with Leena is a huge relief. I didn't want to call her babysitter this close to Christmas and at the last minute. No matter how much I offer to pay, she'd probably quit.

"Thank you, Gabby. Truly. How's Leena?" I ask, dreading the answer.

Gabby hesitates. "She was upset at first, but she understands you have important work to do."

Her words are like a knife to my heart. I've let them both down. "I'm so sorry," I repeat, feeling utterly inadequate. "I'll make it up to you both, I promise."

"Just... just come home when you can, Tyler," Gabby says. "We'll be here."

As I hang up, the weight of everything comes crashing down on me. I've disappointed my boss, potentially jeopardized a major contract, and, worst of all, I've let down the two people who matter most to me. The pressure to be everything to everyone–a successful lawyer, a good father, a reliable partner–feels like it's crushing me.

I run my hands through my hair, feeling the beginnings of a stress headache pounding behind my eyes. How did I let things get so out of control? It feels like everything is slipping through my fingers.

And Gabby... patient, understanding Gabby. How long before her patience runs out?

I shake my head, trying to clear these thoughts. I can't afford to think about that now. I have to fix this mess, have to make things right. But as I turn back to my work, a small voice in the back of my mind whispers a terrifying thought: What if I can't?

The night stretches on, an endless cycle of phone calls, emails, and frantic document revisions. With each passing hour, I feel myself slipping further away from the man I want to be, the father and partner I've been trying to become. The stress builds, a pressure cooker of anxiety and guilt threatening to explode.

As the first light of dawn cracks through the darkness, I stare at my reflection in the computer screen. The man looking back at me is haggard, eyes red-rimmed from lack of sleep, stubble darkening his jaw. He looks nothing like the confident, content man who walked into this office yesterday morning.

I'm right back where I started, prioritizing work over family, letting down the people who matter most.

As I gather my things to head home, exhaustion weighing heavily on my shoulders, I can't shake the feeling that I'm teetering on the edge of a precipice. Something has to give.

These questions swirl in my mind as I step out into the cold morning air, the weight of my failures pressing down on me. I'm terrified of what will happen when I finally break.

Eighteen

TYLER

The warm glow of lights from my house spills onto the snow-covered lawn, creating a deceptively inviting scene. It's that time between dawn and daylight that seems like it's removed from reality. Maybe I'm just too tired to sleep straight–I mean, think straight.

My breath fogs in front of me as I hesitate. The weight of the night's events presses down on me, making each step towards the house feel like I'm wading through molasses.

As I approach the front door, that feeling of sleep hits me–the one where it feels like the house itself went to bed, and you'd better not disturb it until morning. I've become a disturbance in my own home, and I feel like an intruder on the happy holiday. I'm anything but calm and anything but bright.

I turn the key in the lock, the click sounding unnaturally loud in the quiet night. As I step inside, the warmth of the house envelops me, carrying with it the scent of cinnamon and pine. The girls must have baked, and the tree needs water. It's already starting to dry out. In another two weeks, it'll drop needles like snowflakes.

For a moment, I close my eyes and breathe in deeply, trying to find some semblance of peace.

"Daddy!" Leena's excited voice breaks through my reverie. I open my eyes to see her bounding down the stairs, her golden curls bouncing with each step. She's still in her Christmas pajamas, the ones with the dancing reindeer that she insisted on wearing since last Thursday.

I force a smile, kneeling down to catch her as she launches herself into my arms. "Hey, pumpkin. How'd you sleep?"

"We waited for you," she says, her blue eyes wide and earnest. "Where were you?"

"I had to work."

She snuggles into me. "Ms. Robinson read me a bedtime story, but it wasn't the same."

At the mention of Gabby, I look up to see her standing in the doorway to the living room. The soft light from the Christmas tree haloes her chestnut curls, and for a moment, she looks almost angelic. Her hair is just-woke-up, messy and beautiful, and she has a pillow crease on her cheek. I'm struck by the vision that is Gabby.

But then I see the concern in her hazel eyes, the slight furrow of her brow, and guilt washes over me anew.

"Tyler," she says softly, stepping towards us. "We were worried. Is everything okay?"

I stand up, Leena still in my arms, and try to muster

up another smile. "I'm sorry. I didn't want to call and wake everyone up."

Gabby nods, understanding in her eyes. "We had pancakes for dinner. I saved some for you. Would you like me to heat them up?"

The thought of food makes my stomach churn, but I nod anyway. Because having Gabby here, caring for and about me, is worth forcing down some food. I'm sure they're delicious, and once I start eating, the knot in my stomach will go away. "That would be great, thank you."

As Gabby disappears into the kitchen, I carry Leena into the living room. The Christmas tree twinkles in the corner. Presents are piled underneath, some neatly wrapped (Gabby's work, no doubt), others a bit more haphazard (Leena's enthusiastic attempts). The sight of it all–the perfect picture of a family Christmas–makes my chest ache with a mixture of longing and fear.

"Daddy," Leena says, pulling back to look at me. "Are you sad?"

I shake my head, forcing another smile. "No, sweetheart. Just tired."

She nods sagely as if she understands the weight of adult responsibilities. "Ms. Robinson said sometimes grown-ups have to work hard, even when they don't want to. But she said that's why Christmas is special because it's a time for family."

Her innocent words hit me like a punch to the gut. Family. The very thing I've been pushing away, even as I've been desperately trying to create it.

Gabby returns from the kitchen, carrying a plate.

"Here you go," she says, setting the plate on the coffee table. "I hope it's still good..."

She trails off, and I can hear the unspoken words. But you weren't here. But you missed dinner. But you let us down.

"Thank you," I manage to say, my voice sounding rough even to my own ears. "It looks delicious."

Gabby gathers up the blankets she used to sleep to make room for me on the couch, and I fall into the cushions, my body wanting to grow roots and never move. Gabby sits down next to me on the couch, close enough that I can feel the warmth radiating from her body. She reaches out, her hand gently covering mine where it rests on my knee. The touch is meant to be comforting, I know, but it grates on my nerves.

As the warmth of Gabby's hand lingers in mine, a tidal wave of emotions crashes over me, threatening to sweep me away in its turbulent currents. The fear, the doubt, the lingering scars of abandonment–they all converge, forming a perfect storm of insecurity and self-preservation.

Memories of Sarah flash through my mind–the crushing memory of her walking out the door, of her cold words: "You're not providing for me the way I deserve."

In the eye of this emotional hurricane, the voice of reason is drowned out, rendered powerless against the onslaught of past traumas. I'm tense, my neck muscles so tight my scalp hurts.

"Tyler?" Gabby's voice breaks through the tempest in my mind. "Are you sure you're okay? You look pale."

I try to respond, to reassure her, but the words stick in my throat. With each passing moment, the air around me grows thinner, the weight of my emotions pressing down upon me like an invisible force. I feel suffocated, trapped within the confines of my own doubts and fears.

Leena, still perched on my lap, places her small hand on my cheek. "Daddy? Your face is all scrunchy. Are you going to cry?"

Her innocent question is nearly my undoing. In a desperate bid for self-preservation, my instincts scream at me to flee, to retreat to the safety of solitude where no one expects anything from me and no one cares enough that I have to care back. The temptation to isolate myself from the very connections I crave becomes almost overwhelming.

I gently set Leena down on the couch and stand up abruptly, my movements stiff and jerky. "I'm sorry," I manage to choke out. "I... I need some air."

As I turn to leave, the harsh reality of my situation comes crashing down upon me. In my moment of weakness, I have the power to inflict the very pain I have spent a lifetime trying to avoid, to shatter the delicate bonds I have forged with the two women who have brought light into my life.

"Tyler, wait," Gabby says, rising to her feet. "Let's talk about this. Whatever it is, we can–"

But I can't hear the rest of her words. The roaring in my ears drowns out everything else as I stumble towards the door. I grab my coat, not even bothering to put it on, as I wrench open the front door and step out into the cold air.

The biting wind feels like a slap to the face, but it's a welcome sensation compared to the suffocating warmth of the house. I gulp in lungfuls, trying to clear my head to regain some semblance of control.

Behind me, I can hear Gabby's voice, muffled by the closed door. "Leena, sweetheart, why don't you go upstairs and get ready for the day?"

A moment later, the door opens, and I hear Gabby come outside. She doesn't say anything, just stands beside me, her presence a silent offer of support.

For a long moment, we stand there in silence, our breath creating small clouds in the cold air. Finally, I find my voice. "I'm sorry," I say, the words feeling woefully inadequate. "I don't know what came over me."

Gabby's hand finds mine, and she laces our fingers together. "It's okay," she says softly. "We all have moments when it gets to be too much. Do you want to talk about it?"

I shake my head, not trusting myself to speak. The warmth of her hand in mine is both a comfort and a torment, a reminder of everything I want and everything I'm afraid to lose.

"Okay," she says, giving my hand a gentle squeeze. "You don't have to talk. But please, come back inside. It's freezing out here."

I allow her to lead me back into the house, feeling like a puppet whose strings have been cut. As we step back into the warm living room, I see Leena standing at the bottom of the stairs, her eyes wide with worry.

"Daddy?" she says, her voice small and uncertain. "Are you okay now?"

The lump in my throat grows larger. "I'm okay," I manage to say. "I'm sorry if I scared you. Are you ready to get dressed?" She nods and goes up the stairs, her step slow.

She disappears into her room, and I lean against the wall, suddenly exhausted. The events of the night, the emotional turmoil, it all comes crashing down on me at once. I slide down the wall, sitting on the floor with my head in my hands.

I don't know how long I sit there before I feel Gabby's presence beside me. She doesn't say anything, just sits down next to me, her shoulder brushing against mine.

"I'm sorry," I say again, the words muffled by my hands. "You and Leena deserve better than this."

Gabby's hand finds mine, gently pulling it away from my face. "Tyler, look at me," she says softly.

I raise my head, meeting her gaze. The understanding and compassion I see there nearly undoes me.

"We're not going anywhere," she says, her voice firm. "Whatever you're going through, whatever you're feeling, we're here for you. You don't have to face it alone."

Her words, meant to comfort, instead send a fresh wave of panic through me. Because I know, deep down, that I don't deserve this kindness, this unconditional support. That sooner or later, they'll realize it too, and they'll leave, just like Sarah did.

"I... I think I need to be alone for a while," I say, pulling my hand from hers and standing up. "I'm sorry, Gabby. I just... I can't do this right now."

I see the hurt flash in her eyes before she masks it with understanding. "Okay," she says, rising to her feet. "If that's what you need. But Tyler, please remember–you're not alone. When you're ready to talk, I'm here."

I nod, not trusting myself to speak. As Gabby gathers her things and prepares to leave, I feel a mixture of relief and despair. Relief at the prospect of retreating into the familiar comfort of solitude and despair at pushing away the very people who have brought light and warmth back into my life.

As the front door closes behind Gabby, the house feels suddenly empty, the silence oppressive. I make my way to my bedroom.

I sink onto the bed, my head in my hands. The emotions I've been holding at bay all night come crashing over me in waves. Guilt, fear, longing, self-loathing–they swirl together in a toxic mixture.

As the minutes tick by, I find myself drawn to the allure of isolation and the sense of security it offers. I curl up on my bed and fall asleep. Somewhere in the day, Leena climbs up beside me and turns on the television to watch a movie. I drift in and out of sleep, grateful for the numbness it provides.

Nineteen

ROSE

It's Christmas Eve. I can't believe the day has finally come. I've wanted my wings for so long now that it's hard to contain my excitement. My feet are constantly moving, even though I'm sitting in a chair outside of the Great Hall. I'm the first angel to present today, and I'm hours early because I don't have anything else to do but wait.

I smooth down my robes, taking a deep breath to calm my nerves.

I heard the receptionist and the department head talking. The archangel is here. I don't know if he is in the Great Hall or not, but if he is, I'm here. It's difficult to stay in my seat. However, the last thing I want is to start tapping my way around the room, only to draw the archangel out to see what all the ruckus is about.

As I sit-dance, I think about Tyler, Gabby, and Leena. My heart swells with pride at how far they've come. Tyler, once so closed off and afraid to love, now opening his heart to the possibility of family again. Gabby is patient and kind, bringing warmth and music into their lives. And Leena, sweet Leena, whose innocent love has been the catalyst for so much change.

I'm so lost in my thoughts and my dance that I almost don't notice Henry approaching. I sense his presence–a comforting warmth tinged with an undercurrent of... concern?

I flutter to my feet, smoothing my robes once more and trying to compose myself. The closer Henry comes, the easier it is to see the stern set of his mouth, the worry lines creasing his forehead. My heart, which moments ago was soaring with joy, now plummets to my teal blue, patent leather, good luck shoes.

"Rose," Henry says, his voice grave. "You have a problem."

I swallow hard, my mouth suddenly dry. "What do you mean?" I glance at the door, wondering if the archangel is indeed in there or if he was delayed.

Henry shakes his head, his silver hair catching the light. " It's Tyler. He's broken things off with Gabby. Leena is crying in her bed and Tyler... Tyler is settling into being alone again."

I stagger back, my mind reeling. "But... but how?! I don't understand..." I literally left them piled up on his couch like a pile of puppies–warmed by one another and content.

Henry's blue eyes, usually twinkling with mirth, are

now clouded with concern. "The path to love isn't as straightforward as we'd like it to be. Humans are complex, and their hearts are even more so."

I shake my head, disbelief warring with a growing sense of failure. "No, this can't be happening. Not now, not when they were so close!"

"There's still time, but you must act quickly," Henry says, his voice firm but kind. He places a hand on my shoulder, gently but insistently propelling me away from the Great Hall, away from my dissertation, and away from the wings I so desperately want.

I stop and stare at Henry. Time. Time is running out. I press my lips into a thin line. "Henry, if I don't make it back in time, let the next angel go."

He lifts both eyebrows.

"I know. I might miss my chance to present and therefore my wings–" I gulp–" but this is more important. I can try again, but Tyler only gets tonight. It's this Christmas or never for him."

He opens his mouth, and before I know if he's going to protest or tell me to forget the whole thing, I close my eyes and think about Tyler.

"I will, Henry. I promise I won't let them down."

I open my eyes, and I'm in Tyler's home office. His computer screen casts an eerie glow on his haggard face. He looks like he hasn't shaved in days, and his eyes are red. The air here is heavy with the scent of coffee and stress, a far cry from the sweet fragrance of celestial blooms.

Tyler sits hunched over his computer, his fingers flying across the keyboard. The blue light from the screen emphasizes the dark circles under his eyes and the tense set of his jaw. My heart aches at the sight of him, so far removed from the man who was laughing and loving just days ago. A change like this is purposeful. He made a choice, and it took him down this road.

"What have you done?" The words burst from me before I can stop them, filled with a mixture of disappointment and concern.

Tyler spins in his seat, his eyes widening in shock when he sees me. For a moment, he just stares, his mouth opening and closing wordlessly. Then, his surprise gives way to anger.

"What have *I* done?" he repeats, his voice hard. "What have *you* done, Rose? That miracle of yours? It messed everything up. The paperwork was wrong, and now I'm scrambling to fix it before I lose my chance at making partner."

I flinch at his words. "Tyler, I'm so sorry there's an issue. I was trying to help…"

"Help?" He laughs, but there's no humor in it. "You call this helping? I'm drowning."

"What about Leena?" I ask, hoping to pull him from this intense spiral.

"She's asleep," he snaps.

"You think?" I mumble, knowing full well she's in tears. "And Gabby?"

"Gabby's…" he pauses for the briefest of seconds.

"Busy. I'm busy. Life is busy. Anyone who tells you different is trying to sell you beach-front property."

I shake my head, my heart breaking for him, for Gabby, for little Leena. "Tyler, time is the only thing you have to give. It's the most precious gift of all."

He scoffs, turning back to his computer. "Easy for you to say. You're an angel. You probably have all the time in the world."

Time. It's something we angels understand differently than humans. We see the grand tapestry of existence, the way each moment weaves into the next to create a beautiful whole. But humans... they're so caught up in the individual threads that they often miss the bigger picture.

However, that tapestry is accessible and, perhaps, shareable. It's a crazy idea, but it might just work. There's only one way to find out. Moved by a sudden impulse, I step forward and place my hand on Tyler's shoulder. I focus my energy, calling upon my ability to see time. The world around us shimmers and blurs, and suddenly, we're no longer in Tyler's home office. We're in his law firm, watching Tyler from last night, hunched over his computer.

He's still sitting in the chair and blinking as he looks at himself. "That's me," he says in awe. He leans in and then recoils.

"Is this what you want? Is this who you want to be?" I ask.

Tyler turns around in his seat to look up at me. "How did we get here?"

"We're seeing a moment from your past," I explain. "A moment that's shaping your future. You're working so hard, giving so much of yourself to your job. But at what cost?"

I wave my hand and the scene changes. We're in Leena's room now, watching as she sits on her bed, hugging her knees to her chest. Silent tears roll down her cheeks as she stares at a framed photo of her and Tyler.

Tyler's sharp intake of breath tells me he's feeling the impact of this image. "Leena..." he whispers, his voice cracking with emotion.

"She misses you, Tyler," I say gently. "She needs her father in the small moments."

Another wave of my hand, and we're in Gabby's apartment. She's sitting at her piano, her fingers hovering over the keys, but no music plays. Instead, she's staring at her phone, a look of longing and hurt on her face.

"And Gabby," I continue. "She cares for you, Tyler. Deeply. But she can't make you love her, and she values herself enough not to try—even though it's breaking her heart."

Tyler's shoulders slump, the weight of what he's seeing finally hitting him. "Fine, that's my past. What about the future? This has to pay off."

I squeeze his shoulder gently. "A future is nothing without love, Tyler. Without family."

"I'll have time for that. I promise. It'll just be a few more years."

I sigh sadly. "A few years will be too late."

"You don't know that!" he yells at me.

"I can show you." I grab the back of his rolling chair and start running. We're headed for the future, though all Tyler can see is the wall coming up fast.

He throws his hands over his face. "Roooooose!!!"

Twenty

TYLER

I feel the rushing stop. I didn't hit the wall like I expected, and I pull my arms down to see how close I got. I'm at my computer. The past-Tyler is gone, and I'm in his seat.

Weird.

I blink, disoriented, as if waking from a deep sleep. Something feels off, but I can't quite put my finger on it. The air is stale, heavy with the scent of old coffee and neglect.

I glance at the date displayed in the corner of my screen, and my heart nearly stops. December 25th. Christmas Day. But how? Wasn't it just...? I must have fallen asleep at my desk. I roll my neck around. Usually, when that happens, I'm sore and crinkled, but I don't have any problems. That's great.

Except now I missed Christmas morning. The babysitter is going to kill me. Or... I'll end up paying her first semester of tuition.

Panic rising in my throat, I grab my coat and rush out the door, not bothering to shut down the computer. The hallways of the office building are deserted, my footsteps echoing loudly in the emptiness. As I burst through the main doors, the bitter cold of a Christmas morning hits me in the face.

The streets are eerily quiet. No traffic. No one out to greet their neighbor or shovel the walk.

As I approach my house, a sense of unease grows in the pit of my stomach. The windows are dark, no warm glow of Christmas lights or decorations to be seen. It looks... abandoned. Unloved.

I fumble with my keys, my hands shaking from more than just the cold. As I step inside, the silence is deafening. No excited squeals from Leena, no Christmas music playing softly in the background. Just... emptiness.

"Leena?" I call out, my voice sounding strangely hollow in the quiet house. "Leena, where are you?"

There's no response.

"Rose!" I call. "Rose!" She is the last person I remember talking to.

She appears by the fireplace, her hands clasped in front of her.

"Where's Leena?" I demand, panic edging into my voice.

Rose's blue eyes are filled with a sadness that sends a chill down my spine. "She's not here, Tyler," she says softly.

I cross the room and grab her arms; desperation overriding any sense of propriety. "Where is she?" I all but yell, giving her a small shake.

Rose doesn't flinch, her gaze steady and sorrowful. "She's in Cabo San Lucas."

The words don't make sense at first. Cabo San Lucas? On Christmas? "Why is she there?" I ask, my voice barely above a whisper.

Before Rose can answer, my phone rings, startling me. I fumble to answer it, my heart racing.

"Dad?" Leena's voice comes through the speaker, sounding distant and tinny.

"Leena? What are you doing? Where are you?" The questions tumble out in a rush.

"I'm on the beach," she replies, her voice light and carefree.

"The beach? On Christmas?" I stumble over the information.

"This is the best Christmas ever. Thanks for the tickets. Hope you have a good one, Dad. Merry Christmas!"

The call disconnects before I can respond, leaving me staring at the phone in disbelief. I look up, finally taking in my surroundings. The walls are covered with pictures of Leena–her high school graduation and college commencement. Events I have no memory of attending.

"I missed it," I mumble, the realization hitting me like a punch to the gut. "I missed everything." A new fear grips me. "What about Gabby?" I ask Rose, dreading the answer.

"She still lives in town," Rose replies, her voice gentle.

Without another word, I bolt out the door, running towards Gabby's house. The cold air burns my lungs, but I barely notice, focused only on reaching her. As I round the corner onto her street, I skid to a stop, shocked by what I saw.

Gabby's once-charming house now looks neglected, the paint peeling and the garden full of weeds that have withered and been dusted with snow. My heart sinks as I approach, each step feeling heavier than the last. I go through the front gate and approach the porch.

The front door opens, and Gabby steps out onto the porch. "You there? What do you want?" she calls out, her voice wary.

She's still beautiful, still wonderful. But there's a hardness to her now, a wariness that wasn't there before. I move closer, her name escaping my lips in a breath. "Gabby."

I move towards her, but she backs away, her eyes wide with surprise and a hint of fear. "Tyler? What's gotten into you? Are you drunk? You look half-crazy."

Her words sting, but I can't blame her. "I feel like I'm going crazy," I admit, running a hand through my hair. "Can we talk?" I plead, desperation coloring my voice.

Gabby's expression hardens, and she takes a step back. "You made it clear that you didn't want any family, any support, any help. I took your word for it, Tyler." She turns and goes back inside.

I stagger back, feeling as if the ground is crumbling beneath my feet. I spin around, searching for Rose. "I need a miracle," I beg, my voice cracking.

Rose lifts her empty hands, her expression apologetic. "I already used it. I only get one, remember?"

The weight of my choices, of years of pushing people away and focusing on work instead of relationships, comes crashing down on me. I'm consumed by a heavy sense of regret, a gnawing realization that I've pushed away the very people I want to be with. I pushed so hard that they learned to live without me.

I fall to my knees in the snow, the cold seeping through my pants, but I barely notice. Tears burn in my eyes as I look up at the sky, my breath coming out in ragged puffs of white in the cold air.

"Please," I whisper, my voice hoarse with emotion. "Please, I need a second chance. I want my family back. I want to make things right."

The silence that follows is deafening. No heavenly choir, no magical transformation. Just the quiet of a cold Christmas and the crushing weight of my regrets.

I close my eyes, memories flooding my mind. Leena's first steps, her first day of school, her first violin lesson, her first concert, all the moments I missed because I was too busy working. Gabby's warm smile, her patient understanding, and the way she made our house feel like a home. All gone now, slipped through my fingers like sand.

"I'm sorry," I choke out, not sure who I'm apologizing to–Leena, Gabby, myself, or God. Mostly God. "I'm so sorry. I didn't mean for it to be like this. I thought I was doing the right thing, providing for my family, building a future."

I open my eyes, looking at Rose through tears. "Is this really it? Is this what my life becomes? Alone on Christmas, my daughter halfway across the world, the woman I love... lost to me forever?"

Rose kneels beside me, her presence a small comfort. "Tyler," she says gently, "this is a possible future, not a certain one. You still have time to change things, to make different choices."

Her words spark a tiny flame of hope in my chest. "How?" I ask, my voice barely above a whisper. "How do I fix this?"

Rose smiles, a warmth in her eyes that seems to chase away some of the cold. "Choose them. That's it. Choose them first every time."

I nod, a determination growing within me. "I want to do that. I choose Leena. I choose Gabby." I say the words out loud, declaring them as my truth.

As if in response to my words, the world around me begins to shimmer and fade.

Twenty-One

TYLER

I wake up on my bed, the events of the previous night crashing over me like a tidal wave. The weight of regret settles heavy on my chest, making it hard to breathe. I can still see the hurt in Gabby's eyes and hear the disappointment in Leena's voice. How could I have been so blind, so foolish?

I sit up, running a hand through my disheveled hair. The sun is up, and the clock reads almost eleven. I must have slept hard after Rose's trip through time. It almost doesn't seem real, except that I know it happened. I know it as surely as I know that today is Christmas Eve, and I have a lot of begging for forgiveness to do today.

The house is quiet, too quiet. It needs laughter. It needs music. It needs Christmas music. A lot of music.

It needs my girls.

I throw off the covers and rush to Leena's room. I pause outside her door, my hand hovering over the knob. What if I go in there and it's empty like the house was last night? What if I'm stuck in the future I created, and I can't get out?

No. I refuse to believe that.

I chose Leena and Gabby and I'm going to claim them mine.

Take a deep breath and enter.

Leena is already awake, sitting cross-legged on her bed, her favorite stuffed unicorn clutched to her chest. She looks up at me, her blue eyes wary. The sight of her caution breaks my heart all over again.

I rush forward and take her small hands in mine. She's here, and she's little, and she's perfect. I feel like a man reborn. "Merry Christmas!" I kiss her cheek. Then her other one. And then I kiss her face all over until she's laughing and giggling.

"Daddy!" she squeals. I move back, and she's grinning up at me, her eyes bright and merry.

"Leena," I begin. "I'm so sorry. I made some big mistakes with you and with Gabby."

Leena nods. "I miss her."

"Me too. I hurt her feelings, and I hurt your feelings by sleeping all day and then working and not spending time with you. I'm sorry."

Leena's eyes search my face, and I force myself to meet her gaze, to let her see the sincerity in my eyes. "Will you forgive me?"

"Sure," she agrees so readily that I'm humbled. The relief that washes over me is almost dizzying. I pull Leena into a tight hug, breathing in the sweet scent of her strawberry shampoo. "Thank you, sweetheart," I murmur into her hair. "Are you apologizing to Miss Robinson, too?"

"I want to. I think I need to do something for her to show her how sorry I am. What do you think?" I wait. I want Leena involved with this because I want her to see that I care for Gabby and that I want Gabby to be a part of our family.

"She likes crafts," Leena offers.

I nod, trying to wrap my head around any of the crafting ideas and this season. I can't imagine trying to make anything she would actually like–not to mention, I don't have any glitter. "I was thinking we could make her some hot cocoa. She really likes cocoa."

Leena looks up as she thinks. "She likes decorating, too. We should make her an ornament."

I think about Gabby's tree. It's covered with ornaments her students made and gave to her–I can at least do as good of a job as an elementary school kid. "Okay. Let's try."

Leena hops onto her knees, her eyes sparkling with excitement. "Can we put a picture in the ornament?" she asks. "Like a frame?"

I nod, an idea forming. "That's perfect. We can take a new picture every year and make it a tradition."

Just then, my phone rings, the shrill tone cutting through the moment. I glance at the screen–it's my boss. For a split second, old habits threaten to take over, but I push them aside. "It'll just be a minute," I promise Leena as I answer the call. "Why don't you get dressed?"

I walk into the hallway. "Brad," I answer, knowing he isn't one for small talk, anyway. "How are things?"

"You tell me," he barks.

"I've done all I can until I'm back in the office after Christmas." I'm creating boundaries and he's not going to like it. If he fires me, well, then Gabby and I will have a deep conversation about our future. I can sell this house if I have to once we're married. I love being in her home—it feels right. "I feel good about the state of things, and the last time I talked to my client, he was doing well."

"Well?!" Brad's working himself up.

"Brad," I say calmly. "I have to go. I have somewhere I need to be. Merry Christmas."

"Merry—?"

I hang up before he can blow a top. Let the chips fall where they may; I'm not going to worry about it today. Today is about getting my family back together.

Leena busts out of her room as if she's afraid I disappeared on her. I grin at her, and she grins at me.

"What flavor should we make?" I ask as I pull ingredients out. I want to do this right, so I'm scalding a mixture of milk and cream on the stove.

Leena climbs up on a bar stool. "She likes mint." She digs through the flavor packs on the counter until she finds the green one. "Here!"

"Thanks. Will you look through my phone and find a picture of the three of us that we can put on the ornament?" I have some photo paper somewhere in my office to print it on.

She starts scrolling. I turn back to the stove, absently

stirring as I work up my courage to drive over to Gabby's with my chocolate offering and ask her to be a part of our lives. I'm showing up with very little to offer her–I need to give her more. You know, besides all my heart and my future and pride.

Leena hops down and hands me the phone. "This one." I glance at the screen. It's a selfie of the three of us at the parade. "It's perfect. Do you have anything we can make an ornament out of?"

She grins. "I have an ornament." She takes off at a sprint.

The milk starts to steam, and I take it off the burner and add the chocolate pieces. They need to melt, so I take the opportunity to send the image to the printer and load the photo paper. By the time I'm back, the cocoa is almost ready, and Leena's back with a homemade ornament.

"Where did you get that?" I ask.

She looks down. "It's your Christmas present. Do you mind if we give it to Miss Robinson?"

"I don't mind at all. In fact, I think it's the best idea."

We glue the picture on the ornament. It looks like Leena made it, and that's just right. That also means that I really need to get something else for Gabby. I'd ordered her a few gifts, but none of them have the right meaning. I want something that tells her I'm in this for the long haul, and I want us to be a family.

I stir the now-melted chocolate pieces, and the cocoa is ready. I put it in a travel cup, and we're in the car before the glue has a chance to dry.

And I'm still empty-handed.

We drive through town. The streets bustle with last-minute shoppers, people visiting friends and relatives, and a few groups of carolers. The decorations seem brighter, and the sun bounces off the snow.

I want to roll down the windows and yell, "Merry Christmas!" to all I pass.

We slow down as we near the Town Square, and I glance over at Hank's Department Store. There's a group of four mannequins in matching Christmas pajamas. That's it! I yank the wheel, careening into an open parking spot.

"We need one more thing," I tell Leena as we unbuckle and head inside. The store is bright and cheery. I feel bad that the employees are here on Christmas Eve, but the woman who helps us assures us they're off my two and happy to help last-minute shoppers.

She leads us to the pajama section that's been picked over. "It might be difficult to find three matching pairs..."

I wave off her concern. "We'll figure it out. Thank you so much for all your help, and Merry Christmas."

She beams as she hurries off to check someone out.

Leena looks at me as I start digging. "Are these for us?"

I hand her two pairs in my size and start looking for matching sets. "For us and Gabby." I hand her one in what I think is Gabby's size. "I want her to know she belongs with us." I stop and turn to Leena. "Are you okay with that? If she's part of our family?"

Leena bounces on her toes and hugs the pajamas to her chest. "Yes!"

I wish my heart was as easy to open as Leena's. She's so full of love it spills out of her. I give her a hug. It doesn't take long to find a full set of three pairs of pajamas. A few minutes later, we emerge with a bag and a plan.

As we approach Gabby's house, my heart begins to race. Leena clutches the ornament and the bag of pajamas, her face a picture of determination. Maybe I should have done this on my own and saved her from the possible rejection that's headed my way, but I couldn't see making us a family without including Leena.

We arrive, and I climb out immediately, so I don't have time to think about what I'm doing. I know this is the right thing to do. I know I love Gabby, and she's the only person who can complete our circle. I just hope she knows all those things, too.

We reach the front door, and suddenly, I'm paralyzed with doubt. Is this too much? Not enough? Should I have brought flowers? A box of chocolates?

Leena gives my hand a reassuring squeeze. "Don't worry, Daddy," she says with the wisdom of a child. "Ms. Robinson will love it. She loves us."

Before I can respond, Leena starts singing. Her sweet voice rings out in an impromptu rendition of *We Wish You a Merry Christmas*. After a moment of surprise, I join in, my voice wavering with emotion as we pour our hearts into the festive melody.

The door opens and there stands Gabby. Her curls

are slightly mussed, and her eyes are rimmed with red—evidence of a sleepless night or tears? Dare I hope that she's been missing us as much as we've been missing her?

Leena and I go in for a big finish, and I throw my arms out to the sides and wave my hands.

Gabby claps politely. "Hi, you two," she says, her voice a mixture of confusion and hope.

Leena hands her the ornament. "We made this for you."

Gabby takes it carefully. She studies the picture, her eyes filling with tears.

I take a deep breath, steeling myself. "Gabby, I came to apologize. I was an idiot. I let my fears and insecurities get the best of me, and I pushed you away. But the truth is, I don't want to push you away. I want you in my life, in our lives."

I hand her the cocoa and then take the bag out of Leena's hands. "We brought you some things. They're not much, but..."

Before I can finish, Gabby sets the gifts on her entry table, steps forward, and wraps her arms around me. The warmth of her embrace, the forgiveness in her touch, nearly brings me to my knees.

"Tyler," she murmurs, her voice thick with emotion. "I was so worried. I thought..."

"I know," I interrupt gently, pulling back to meet her gaze. "I'm so sorry, Gabby. I've been afraid for so long–afraid of being hurt, afraid of letting anyone in. But I don't want to be afraid anymore. I want to be brave enough to love you, to let you love us." I brush a piece of hair off her cheek.

Gabby's eyes fill with tears, but she's smiling. "Tyler," she whispers, and then she's kissing me. It's soft and sweet and tastes like forgiveness and new beginnings.

When we part, I'm aware of Leena bouncing excitedly beside us. "Ms. Robinson!" she exclaims. "You need to open your presents! We got matching pajamas, and we're going to take a picture for the ornament and make it a tradition and–"

Gabby laughs, bending down to hug Leena. She meets my eyes over Leena's head, and I can see the love and joy shining there. The surprise of the matching pajamas may be ruined, but it doesn't matter. Nothing matters except this moment, this feeling of rightness and belonging.

As we step inside Gabby's house, that is warm and inviting. I feel a sense of peace settle over me. This is where I belong. This is what matters. Work, success, money–they all pale in comparison to the love and joy I feel right now.

Leena tugs on my hand, her eyes shining with excitement. "Can we put on our pajamas now, Daddy? And take the picture?"

I look at Gabby, who nods with a smile. "I think that's a wonderful idea," she says.

I laugh, feeling lighter than I have in years. "That sounds perfect," I agree. "Then we can have some hot chocolate. It's getting cold."

As we settle in, sipping cocoa and laughing over

Leena's enthusiasm for our new matching pajamas, I can't help but marvel at how quickly everything has changed. Just yesterday, I was lost in a world of spreadsheets and legal briefs, missing out on the true joys of life.

But now, watching Gabby help Leena add whipped cream to her cocoa and hearing their shared laughter, I know I've found something far more valuable than any career success. I've found family. I've found love. I've found home.

And as we gather in front of Gabby's fireplace, dressed in our matching pajamas and smiling for the camera, I make a silent vow. I will never again take this for granted. I will cherish every moment, every laugh, every shared look. Because this–this right here–is what Christmas is truly about. It's about family, love, and the joy of being together.

The camera flashes, capturing this perfect moment. And as I look at Gabby and Leena, their faces alight with happiness, I know that this is just the beginning. We have a lifetime of Christmases ahead of us, a lifetime of new traditions and shared memories.

And I can't wait for every single one of them.

Epilogue

ROSE

The light in the Grand Hall pulses with a soft, golden glow as I stand in the spotlight at the lecturn. Henry and the Archangel sit behind a desk, waiting for me to present my dissertation on guardian angel-ship.

Two days ago, I was so sure I was going to get my wings that I could have floated through this moment without a worry. Now, I'm not so sure. I mean, Tyler definitely found the spirit of family and is on his way to a wonderful life. The thing is, I've learned a little bit about myself, too, and I'm not sure how that's going to play into getting my wings.

Henry's kind eyes meet mine, his silver hair catching the light. The Archangel Saint Nicolas, sitting beside him, exudes an aura of power and wisdom that both awes and humbles me. I take a deep breath, steeling myself for what's to come. The cool marble floor beneath my feet grounds me, and I resist the urge to break into a nervous tap dance.

"Rose," Henry says, his voice warm and encouraging, "we're ready. Please, begin."

I close my eyes for a moment, centering myself and seeking divine guidance before I begin to speak.

"Fellow Angels," I begin, my voice fills the hall in a way I'm not used to and I startle at the sound of it. I clear my throat and continue on. "Before this assignment, I viewed my duties through a narrow lens. I thought that progress was all forward, not taking into account that sometimes people slide backward so they can recognize what they're leaving behind."

I hope this makes sense. The memories of my time on Earth flood my senses–the crisp winter air of Benton Falls, the warmth of Gabby's smile, the sound of Leena's laughter. These experiences have changed me in ways I'm only beginning to understand, deepening my appreciation for God's intricate design in every human life.

"Too often, I got caught up in the logistics, focusing solely on ensuring that things run smoothly for Tyler. I used a miracle card to lighten his workload in the fastest way possible. I thought I was removing a stumbling block for him, not knowing that it would cause problems later." I pause and think over my next words. "I'm not sure how things would have been if Tyler still felt buried. Maybe he would have realized Leena needs him, and Gabby loves him, maybe not. But I realized that my true purpose as a guardian angel is to guide humans toward greater peace, happiness, and love–to help them feel the embrace of our Heavenly Father."

I pause, letting the weight of these words sink into my own soul.

I can't help but think of James, the doctor who did not enjoy being a janitor. He's thriving in the role of guidance counselor. He hardly leaves the office because he doesn't want anyone to arrive and not be greeted. He's going to do a wonderful job, and I encouraged him to begin training as a guardian as soon as possible. When one follows their passion, even the most daunting tasks can become a labor of love.

"What did you learn from this assignment?" asks Henry.

I draw in a breath and gather my thoughts. "Tyler taught me that family is not just a bond of blood, but a bond forged through compassion, vulnerability, and faith. His initial resistance stemmed from the trauma of abandonment–a legitimate fear that prevented him from opening his heart. But through his journey, I was reminded that no one is ever truly lost or alone to Him who created them. God's love is constant, unwavering, and eternal."

Now, I can see how God's love was present even in those dark moments, waiting patiently for Tyler to recognize it. And, as I think back to my own struggles as a guardian angel in training, there were times I felt lost or unsure even as God was guiding me along, preparing me for this very moment.

"What will you do if you do not get your wings?" Henry asks curiously.

I gulp. It's always a possibility. There are many angels who don't pass on their first try. There's no shame here as long as we're learning and growing.

"If required to stay in my current role, I will approach each new angel with fresh eyes and an open heart. I will seek to understand their unique gifts and propensities so that I might place them in positions that feed their souls as well as their duties. For we are all unique creations of God, each with our own special purpose in His grand design."

I make eye contact with Henry as I say this, silently thanking him for his patience throughout my training. His eyes twinkle with pride, and I feel a surge of affection for my mentor.

"Very good. Please give us a moment to consult." Henry turns to Saint Nicholas, and their heads come together as they whisper.

I stand there, my toes thrumming against the floor. I say a silent prayer, entrusting myself to God's will.

Finally, they stop whispering, and Henry stands. His face is solemn, but I can see a hint of a smile tugging at the corners of his mouth. He reaches out and grasps a golden bell that seems to materialize out of thin air. The sight of it sends a thrill of excitement through me. Oh my goodness!

With a gentle movement, Henry rings the bell. The sound that emanates from it is unlike anything I've ever heard–a pure, clear tone that seems to resonate with the very fabric of Heaven itself. As the sound washes over me, I feel a tingling sensation spreading through my body.

"Rose," Henry's voice is filled with warmth and pride, "it is my great pleasure to announce that you have earned your wings. You are now a full-fledged guardian angel."

The words barely have time to register before I feel it–a rush of power and light emanating from within me. I gasp as my new wings stretch out behind me in a glorious display of celestial beauty.

Saint Nicholas appears at my side and places a hand on my shoulder. The touch sends a surge of energy through me, cementing my new status.

"Well done, Rose," he says; his voice is like a symphony, complex and beautiful. "You have learned the true meaning of your calling well. Go forth and continue to spread God's love, comfort, and the Spirit of Family among humanity."

Overwhelmed with emotion, I can't help myself. My feet begin to move, and before I know it, I'm tap dancing right there in the Grand Hall of Heaven. My new wings shimmer and sparkle in time with my movements, creating a dazzling display of light and motion.

Henry and the Archangel are smiling widely, clearly amused and touched by my exuberant display.

As I dance, I think of Tyler, Gabby, and little Leena. I think of the family they've become, the love they've found. And I know, with a certainty that goes beyond mere knowledge, that this is what it's all about. This is why we do what we do–to help God's children find their way back to Him, to each other, to love.

And now, with my wings and all the knowledge I've gained, I'm ready to help them all.

Continue reading for a glimpse into Angel Institute Book 2: Ren.

Spend more time with angels in training this Christmas!

Angel Institute Book 2

CHAPTER 1

Arthur

I take a deep breath, savoring the sweet scent of blooming jasmine mixed with the clear, heavenly air. The celestial classroom looks the same as ever, but today feels different. Ten of us sit in rows. The room itself is an ethereal masterpiece, with walls that shimmer like the dawn sky, painted in hues of gold and silver. The ceiling is a vast, open expanse, dotted with twinkling stars that cast a gentle glow over everything. Plush, cloud-like chairs cradle us as we sit at polished wooden desks, their surfaces etched with symbols of wisdom and learning.

I shift in my seat, wondering if I'll ever get used to these robes. My name is Arthur, and while I was often mistaken for Santa Claus during my time on earth, I usually prefer plants to people—and that's what's got me worried about this final assignment.

Henry, our mentor, stands at the front of the classroom. He's got blue eyes, silver hair that's always a bit messy, and he wears robes that shimmer with celestial light. His calm, reassuring voice pairs well with his majestic wings, which are folded gracefully behind him.

"Welcome, my dear trainees," Henry says, looking at each of us in turn. "Today is a big day. Each of you will receive a letter with your final assignment on Earth. You have until midnight on Christmas Eve to fulfill your mission, and then you'll return here to give a dissertation on your experience. Pass, and you'll earn your wings."

I try to swallow the lump in my throat. Leaving the serenity of the heavenly gardens to interact with humans feels like being asked to swap garden shears for social skills—two things I've never been good at. And those wings... I glance at Henry's and silently pray that I can earn my own. I've heard whispers about Enoch's Garden —only accessible with wings — filled with plants I could only dream of, and I long to tend to them.

Henry keeps talking, weaving in stories and metaphors like he always does. He tells us about the importance of learning through experience and making mistakes. His words are filled with old proverbs and classic literature quotes, adding a touch of timeless wisdom to his lessons.

Betty, sitting next to me, leans over and whispers, "I hope mine involves something simple. I'm still getting used to making these robes."

"Knowing you, Betty, it'll be something that requires a lot of heart," I reply, managing a small smile. Her deep brown eyes are filled with warmth despite her worries.

Gabe, the rugged ex-cattle rancher on my other side, chuckles. "Well, if I get another job that involves fixing halos, I might just start a rebellion."

"Maybe you'll get to ride bulls on Earth," I suggest, my attempt at humor making him laugh.

Henry hands out the letters one by one. When he gets to me, his eyes soften. He places the letter in my hand and squeezes my shoulder.

"Arthur, your time has come," Henry says warmly. "Remember, your strength lies in your patience and kindness. Trust yourself and what you've learned."

I nod, but my stomach churns as I look at the letter in my hand. Patience and kindness were never my strong suit during my time on earth. The parchment feels both fragile and heavy. As Henry moves on to Mary, the nurturing, motherly figure with her golden brown hair and serene demeanor, I take a deep breath and open my letter.

Dear Celestial Trainee,

Your final examination has arrived. This Christmas season, you are tasked with a mission of utmost importance—one that will determine your readiness to receive your wings and ascend to the honored rank of guardian angel.

You are hereby assigned to assist:

Police Officer Ren Michaels

Your objective is to help this individual discover and embrace the true spirit of friendship this Christmas. This task will require all the skills and compassion you have cultivated during your training at the Angel Institute.

Remember, you will be evaluated based on your ability to guide and inspire without direct intervention. Your success hinges on [Human's Name]'s genuine understanding and application of this essential Christmas virtue.

Be advised: the stakes are high. A successful mission will earn you your wings and the privilege of becoming a guardian angel. However, failure to complete this task satisfactorily will result in a century-long delay before you may attempt this final test again.

May the light of Heaven guide you in this crucial endeavor. We have the utmost faith in your abilities.

Wishing you divine success,

The Angelic High Council

I chuckle nervously to myself. "A police officer?" I think. "Teaching a cactus to be friendly might be easier." A couple of scenes from my time on earth flash in my mind, a handful of times when the law and I seemed to be on different sides of the fence.

Anxiety gnaws at me. This task feels monumental. This will require me to talk to a human, to care about their interests and concerns, *rrrr*. I worry all the hours spent practicing in the classroom haven't prepared me for what's ahead.

Rebecca, our reluctant resident weather forecaster, receives her assignment with a dramatic sigh. "Hmph." She scrunches her nose. "The spirit of giving. At least I might not have to use the words 'sunny and warm' for a week or two."

Lillian, candy-loving as ever, grins as she reads hers. "Looks like I'll be guiding lost souls. Wonder if I can use lollipops as bribes?"

Gladys, ever the tinkerer, giggles. "This'll be fun! Can't wait to start fixing."

John adjusts his colorful socks, a habit he does when he's nervous. "I've got a journalist," he says, wiggling his toes to show off the vibrant patterns. "Maybe he'll want to do a story about my socks."

Henry wraps up with a final piece of advice. "Remember, you are not alone. I'm always here if you've got questions."

We all nod and rise from our seats, ready to start our missions.

"And don't forget about the Miracle Card and the Blessings Hotline." Henry adds as we step out of the classroom and into the bustling hallway of the Angel Institute building.

I hold the letter close, feeling the weight of responsibility and an unexpected shock of excitement. Ren is waiting and I've got a chance to earn my wings.

"Okay, Arthur," I mutter to myself, "time to face the music. Let's hope my green thumb works on humans, too."

Pushing through the doors, I sigh as warmth and light wrap around me. I plan to take one more look at my garden before I leave, but unexpectedly, I'm overcome with this feeling of urgency to begin my assignment as quickly as possible, as if there is something I'm needed to do—and it can't wait.

I close my eyes, think of Ren and the possibility of what is coming and suddenly...

To continue reading, grab book 2 in The Angel Institute Christmas Series.

The angels in training are waiting for you!
Enjoy all the Christmas stories that fill your heart with holiday joy.

Acknowledgments

Writing a book is never a solitary endeavor, and we are profoundly grateful for the incredible team of individuals who have supported us throughout this journey.

First and foremost, we want to express our heartfelt thanks to our amazing beta readers: Rolayne, Marissa, and Renee. Your keen insights, thoughtful feedback, and unwavering enthusiasm have been invaluable. You truly are the best beta readers we could have hoped for, and this series is better because of your contributions.

A special thank you goes to Richard for his meticulous consistency read. Your eagle eye for detail and ability to catch those elusive inconsistencies that somehow slip through have been instrumental in polishing our work to a shine.

We are deeply appreciative of Shaylee for her unwavering support and for helping us launch the Angels Unscripted podcast. Your creativity and dedication have opened up new avenues for us to connect with our readers and share the world of the Angel Institute.

To our wonderful reviewers, we cannot thank you enough. Your thoughtful words and enthusiasm for our books have been a constant source of motivation. Your efforts in spreading the word about the Angel Institute series have been crucial in helping us reach new readers. We are truly grateful for your support and advocacy.

Lastly, to our readers – thank you for embarking on this heavenly adventure with us. Your love for our characters and stories makes all the late nights and rewrites worthwhile.

This series is a labor of love, made possible by the collective efforts of many. We are blessed to have such an incredible community surrounding us, and we thank you all from the bottom of our hearts.

Book Club Questions

Hello, fellow readers!

We're excited you've chosen *Angel Institute: Your Assignment: Tyler* for your book club. Now that you've journeyed through Tyler's struggles as he learn to cherish family at Christmas, it's time to dive deeper into the heart of the story.

These questions are designed to get you thinking about the bigger picture—the themes, character arcs, and those "aha!" moments that made the story come alive.

Whether you're pondering the challenges faced by our guardian angels in training or dissecting the complexities of human nature, we hope these questions will enrich your reading experience and lead to some enlightening discussions.

So grab your favorite beverage, settle in with your book club, and let's explore the heavenly and earthly realms of Angel Institute together. Happy discussing!

- How does Tyler's relationship with work evolve throughout the story? What causes these changes?
- Discuss the role of Rose as a guardian angel. How effective is she in guiding Tyler towards a better life?
- How does Leena's character influence Tyler's growth and decision-making?
- Analyze the development of Tyler and Gabby's relationship. What obstacles do they face, and how do they overcome them?
- How does the theme of family manifest itself throughout the novel? How does Tyler's understanding of family change?
- Discuss the significance of Christmas in the story. How does the holiday season impact the characters and plot?
- How does Tyler's past, particularly his experience with Sarah, affect his ability to form new relationships?
- Analyze the use of time travel in the story. How does it impact Tyler's perspective and choices?
- How does the author portray the balance between career success and personal relationships? Do you agree with this portrayal?
- Discuss the role of forgiveness in the novel. How do different characters demonstrate or struggle with forgiveness?

- How does the concept of divine intervention play out in the story? Do you think it's handled effectively?
- Analyze the character of Gabby. How does she complement or challenge Tyler?
- Discuss the symbolism of Tyler's work miracle. What does it represent, and what are its consequences?
- How does the author explore the theme of vulnerability throughout the novel?
- Discuss the role of community in the story. How does Tyler's relationship with his town change?
- How does the novel portray the process of personal growth and change? Is it realistic?
- Analyze the use of music and creativity in the story, particularly through Gabby's character.
- How does the author handle the concept of second chances? Are they earned or freely given?
- Discuss the portrayal of Heaven and celestial beings in the novel. How does it compare to other depictions you've encountered?
- By the end of the novel, do you believe Tyler has truly changed? Why or why not?

About the Author

Lucy McConnell loves Cadbury Mini Eggs, Elvis, and Christmas. She believes that clean romance books should keep you up past your bedtime, bring smiles and laughter to your day, and have happy endings.

With that in mind, she's written over 140 novels full of fun and flirty characters who navigate the turbulent waters of romance with open hearts and creativity.

If you enjoy romance stories with great kissing scenes, check out her website at GelatoPublishing.com.

Also by Lucy McConnell

The Marrying Miss Kringle Series

The Reindeer Wrangler Ranch Series

The Harvest Ranch Romance Series

Mission: Harvest Ranch Wedding Series

The Diamond Cove Series

The Brides Wanted Matchmaker Series

Billionaire Bachelor Cove

Dating Mr. Baseball

Texas Titans Romances

And more!

Milton Keynes UK
Ingram Content Group UK Ltd.
UKHW020106181024
449757UK00012B/730